W9-BGD-903

The Case of the Booby-Trapped Pickup

The Case of the
Booby-Trapped Pickup

John R. Erickson

Illustrations by Gerald L. Holmes

Viking

VIKING
Published by Penguin Group
Penguin Young Readers Group, 345 Hudson Street,
New York, New York 10014, U.S.A.
Penguin Group (Canada), 90 Eglinton Avenue East, Suite 700, Toronto, Ontario,
Canada M4P 2Y3 (a division of Pearson Penguin Canada Inc.)
Penguin Books Ltd, 80 Strand, London WC2R 0RL, England
Penguin Ireland, 25 St Stephen's Green, Dublin 2, Ireland
(a division of Penguin Books Ltd)
Penguin Group (Australia), 250 Camberwell Road, Camberwell, Victoria 3124,
Australia (a division of Pearson Australia Group Pty Ltd)
Penguin Books India Pvt Ltd, 11 Community Centre, Panchsheel Park,
New Delhi - 110 017, India
Penguin Group (NZ), 67 Apollo Drive, Mairangi Bay, Auckland 1310, New Zealand
(a division of Pearson New Zealand Ltd)
Penguin Books (South Africa) (Pty) Ltd, 24 Sturdee Avenue, Rosebank,
Johannesburg 2196, South Africa

Registered Offices: Penguin Books Ltd, 80 Strand, London WC2R 0RL, England

Published simultaneously in the United States of America by Viking
and Puffin Books, divisions of Penguin Young Readers Group, 2007

1 3 5 7 9 10 8 6 4 2

Copyright © John R. Erickson, 2007
All rights reserved

LIBRARY OF CONGRESS CATALOGING-IN-PUBLICATION DATA
Erickson, John R.
The case of the booby-trapped pickup / by John R. Erickson ;
illustrations by Gerald L. Holmes.
p. cm. — (Hank the cowdog ; 49)
Summary: Hank the Cowdog, Head of Ranch Security, almost
loses his job after two fiasco-filled rides in Slim's pickup truck.
ISBN 978-0-670-06186-0 (hardcover) — ISBN 978-0-14-240755-4 (pbk.)
[1. Dogs—Fiction. 2. Ranch life—Texas—Fiction. 3. Texas—Fiction.
4. Humorous stories.] I. Holmes, Gerald L., ill. II. Title.
PZ7.E72556Cacc 2007
[Fic]—dc22
2006031313

Hank the Cowdog® is a registered trademark of John R. Erickson.

Printed in the United States of America

*For Bert Bostic of Midland, Texas,
and his spectacular Spirit Wind choirs*

CONTENTS

The Case of the
Booby-Trapped Pickup

CHAPTER ONE

A Hairy Witch
Invades the Ranch

It's me again, Hank the Cowdog. A coyote that came into the feed ground and ate with the cows? Ridiculous. Impossible. I didn't believe one word of Slim's story until . . . well, until I saw that coyote with my own eyes and she turned out to be a gorgeous princess who fell madly in love with me.

But that comes later in the story. Forget I mentioned it.

Where were we? Oh yes, the mystery began in the wintertime, as I recall, the first part of winter, maybe late November, because I had recently switched the ranch over to our Winter Routine.

Have we discussed the WR? Maybe not. The

1

Winter Routine is the routine we follow in the winter, and that's why we call it...maybe this is obvious, but it's not so obvious what we do in the Winter Routine. Are you ready to hear this? Pay attention.

First thing, we send all the summer birds packing, your sparrows, larks, cardinals, robins, tweeties, and so-forth birds. Sometime in September or October, we give 'em the order to move out and fly south. Why? Because after putting up with them all summer, I'm ready to clean house and get 'em off the ranch.

I mean, you talk about noisy! Around here, a dog can hardly sleep in the summertime for all the noise. They tweet, twitter, squeak, squawk, chirp, and chatter from sunup to sundown, and some of 'em don't quit at sundown. They tweet and twitter half the night. Annoying? You bet.

Another thing that annoys me is that they nest in ranch trees without permission. If they showed some respect and asked my permission, I'd probably give it. I mean, birds have to do *something.* They don't have honest jobs, so they need a place to loiter and do their little nothings. But they don't ask permission. They just move in, take over ranch trees, and start making noise. That really burns me up.

On your average summer day, I have to spend an hour and fifteen minutes barking at the little dummies and trying to restore law and order. The Head of Ranch Security shouldn't have to get involved with such silliness, but if I didn't do it, who would? Barking at birds would make a nice little summer job for Drover, but he can't be trusted. His mind wanders, you know.

But the point is that by the middle of September, I'm sick of birds and I give 'em the order to shove off. You know what? It works every time. Those birds pack up their feathers and head south in droves, and we don't see 'em again until the following spring. Pretty impressive, huh? You bet. Those birds don't want to mess with the Head of Ranch Security.

The other part of the Winter Routine comes when I issue a directive to ranch employees: "Attention please! The Security Division has been monitoring the nutritional needs of our cattle, and as of yesterday afternoon, the protein level of our pasture grass dropped below the minimum. Therefore, tomorrow morning all cowboys will initiate our Winter Feeding Program and will continue feeding until I issue another directive next spring. Any employees who don't understand this directive, or who don't agree with it, are invited to follow orders and keep their traps shut."

Are you surprised that a dog would be so deeply involved in the ranch's Winter Feeding Program? Most of your ordinary ranch mutts don't, but me . . . well, as I always say, no task is too small to be little.

No task is too small to be big.

No task is too big to belittle.

No task is too . . . there's a neat old saying that captures what I'm trying to say here, but at the moment . . . just skip it.

Where were we? Oh yes, winter had come to the ranch and I had put our Winter Routine into action, which meant that we were . . . well, ready for winter. We had swept out another crop of pesky little tweet-tweets and I had ordered the cowboy crew back to work, feeding cattle every day. I knew they hated that, I mean, they had spent most of the summer tacking up fence and tearing up equipment in the alfalfa patch, goofing off and playing so-called practical jokes on us dogs, and now they had to load up sacks of feed every morning and actually do some work on the ranch.

I heard them grumbling and complaining, but it didn't soften my heart one bit. By George, I had sent down my orders and that was the end of it.

Well, almost. On the morning of November 28, the very first day of winter feeding, a problem developed, a problem so serious that even I hadn't antipisated it. At 8:07 that morning . . . anticipated . . . at 9:07 that morning, Slim's old pickup quit working. It died right in front of the machine shed, and we're talking about graveyard dead.

Fortunately, I was on duty and ready to swing into action. Whilst Slim raised the hood and went through his usual checklist (scratching his head, scowling at the motor, wiggling two wires, and calling the pickup a piece of junk), I reached for the microphone of my mind and put out a call to the Elite Troops of the Security Division.

"Hank to Drover, over. Report to the machine shed at once. We've got a mechanical failure up here, and Slim's in over his head, over. Do you copy?"

I waited and listened. Not a sound, except for static on the radio. Where was he? Every time I really needed the little goof, he was . . . but then I heard the shuffle of his feet on the gravel, and he came dragging around the northeast corner of the machine shed. Was he running or showing any indication that this was an urgent matter? No.

He was taking his sweet time, wearing a silly grin and gazing around at the scenery.

He walked into the icy beam of my hot glare and stopped. "Oh, hi. Were you barking for me?"

"I called you, yes. You may have thought I was merely barking, but it was actually a downlink microwave transmission from one of the Security Division's communication satellites."

"I'll be derned. It sure sounded like a bark to me."

"It was more than a bark, but never mind. Did you get my urgent message?"

"Well, let me think here." He rolled his eyes around. "I think you said that Slim was . . . standing on his head?"

The air hissed out of my lungs. "That wasn't the message. I said that Slim was *in over* his head. His pickup quit on him and he needs backup right away."

"His pickup won't back up?"

"Affirmative. It won't back up and it won't go forward either. It's broken and he needs a backup from us."

"You mean . . . we have to pull it backward?"

I stuck my nose in his face. "Drover, listen to me. The pickup won't start and Slim is a lousy

6

mechanic. He needs our help. Do you under-stand?"

"Well . . . I'm not sure. How come he's standing on his head?"

"He's not standing on his head! Look at him. Is he standing on his head?"

You won't believe this part. Just as Drover swung his gaze around, Slim bent down and looked underneath the pickup, so that his head almost touched the ground. Drover flashed a grin. "Oh, I see now. He's standing on his head, trying to figure out how come the pickup won't back up, only he's not really standing on his head. Did I get it right?"

What can you say? "Yes. Fine. Very good. Now, let's march over there and see if we can lend a hand."

"What if we don't have any hands?"

I froze. "What?"

"If all you've got is paws, how can you lend a hand?"

"Drover, are you trying to be funny?"

"I don't think so. All I've got is four paws, honest. See?" He proceeded to show me his paws.

"Then *don't* lend a hand. Lend a paw. Let's go. We're wasting valuable time here." I shoved my way past him and started toward Slim.

"Which paw?"

Again, I had to stop. "What did you say?"

"When?"

"Just now."

He rolled his eyes around. "Well, let me think. I said that Slim was standing on his head."

"No, after that."

"Well, I said . . . I already forgot."

I could feel my temper rising. "You said . . . you said something about a witch."

"I did?"

"Yes, you certainly did, and don't try to deny it. Now, why were you inquiring about witches?"

His eyes blanked out. "I don't know, but Halloween's already past."

"That's correct. Are you saying that we still have a Halloween witch running around on the ranch?"

"Well . . ."

"Because, if you are"—I began pacing in front of him—"this could lead our investigation into an entirely new direction."

"Yeah, but . . ."

"Where did you see this witch? Around head-quarters?"

"No, all I said was, which paw?"

I froze in my tracks. "Witch paw? She had paws? Holy smokes, Drover, why didn't you report this sooner?"

"No, I said . . ."

"A witch with paws! This could turn out to be very interesting." I resumed my pacing. "Okay, let's follow up on this. Describe the paws."

He held up a foot and squinted at it. "Well, let's see. Four toes and dirty nails, and hair between the toes."

"Ah! Now we're getting somewhere. This was a *hairy* witch, the most dangerous kind. Was she riding a broom? Carrying a pumpkin? Did she have a black cat?" I noticed that the runt had collapsed to the ground and covered his ears with his paws. I marched over to him. "Now what? I'm trying to work up this case, Drover, but I must have your cooperation. Was she riding a broom?"

"Who?"

"The witch, of course."

He let out a moan. "I didn't see a witch! I don't know what you're talking about!"

"You . . . you didn't see a hairy witch with paws?"

"No!"

There was a long moment of silence. "Drover, if you didn't see a witch, then what is the point of this conversation?"

"I don't know. I'm so confused, I want to go back to bed."

"I see." I took a slow breath of air. "In that case . . . Drover, what were we doing before you dragged us into a ridiculous conversation about witches?"

"I don't remember."

"Hmmm. Neither do I." I sat down and began scratching my right ear. A moment later, I heard Slim scream, "Piece of junk!" And it all came rushing back. I leaped to my feet and called Drover to action, and we sprinted over to help Slim in his hour of greatest need.

A Terrible
Explosion

Did you understand any of that business about the witch? I never figured it out, but when you work around Drover, you have to expect a certain amount of chaos and nonsense. But the important thing is that we were able to rush two loyal dogs to the scene of Slim's latest crisis.

We got there just in time. Slim's face had turned red. There was fire in his eyes and his lips were pulled back in a snarl of rage. He held a ball-peen hammer in his right hand and, well, I got the impression that he was ready to throw it through the windshield.

"Okay, Drover, let's set the formation. It's obvious that Slim needs our help."

"Gosh, what'll we do?"

"What do you think? We bark, of course, but not ordinary barks. For this deal, we'd better go to Motor Tune-up Barks. Ready? Let 'er rip!"

Boy, you should have been there. It was really something to see and hear—two brave dogs pouring heart and soul into a chorus of barking against rust, corrosion, sludge, and your other evil agents that cause pickups to quit running. I don't know as we'd ever done a better job with the Motor Tune-up Program, and I think it would have worked if only . . .

I guess Slim didn't understand what we were doing. (How many times has that happened? Thousands of times.) Maybe he thought we were just barking, just a couple of dumb mutts yapping at nothing in particular. In other words, he missed the whole point of the Motor Tune-up Barking Procedure. Just about the time we had really gotten into a rhythm and were pumping out some outstanding barks, he whirled around and screeched, "Knock off the dadgum noise, will you?"

HUH? Knock off the . . .

Okay. Fine. Sure. If that's the way he felt about it, you bet, we could sit there like knots on a log and let his dumb old pickup rot into the ground. I mean, I had plenty of things to do and didn't need to take his insults. If he thought he could fix his rattletrap piece-of-junk pickup without help from his dogs, by George, that was fine with me.

I turned to my assistant. "Okay, Drover, let's shut 'er down. Our help isn't wanted here."

"Oh, darn. I was just getting into the good part."

"I know, but we can't help him if he doesn't want to be helped. We'll just have to let him learn the hard way. Mark my words, son, they'll have to tow that pickup all the way into town and leave it with a mechanic."

"Gosh, that's too bad. You reckon we could have fixed it?"

"Oh, sure, no question about it. Two more minutes of barking would have done the trick. But don't be discouraged. We did all two dogs could have done. Let's get out of here."

I gave Slim one last wounded glance and started to leave, but just then Loper came walking up from the house. I figured we might as well stick around and witness the next chapter in the drama.

Loper walked up to the front of the pickup and looked under the hood. "Problem?"

Slim nodded and gestured with the hammer. "Yalp, but if you'll leave for about five minutes and cover your ears, I think I can fix it."

"What's the trouble?"

"Won't start."

"It's probably flooded. I smell gasoline."

"It's a piece of junk."

Loper gave his head a shake. "Slim, some of us have the talent to fix machinery and some don't. You couldn't fix a yo-yo if the string broke."

"Yeah? Then start it yourself."

"I will. The secret is, don't pump the foot-feed."

"I didn't."

"That floods the motor." Loper opened the pickup door and sat behind the wheel. "Watch and study your lessons, Slimbo." Loper turned the key and cranked the motor. He cranked it for two minutes and nothing happened.

A lopsided smirk spread across Slim's mouth. "Don't quit now. You've still got some battery left."

Loper showed him the palm of his hand. "Patience. That was just Step One. Did you open up the carburetor?"

Slim hitched up his jeans. "No, I didn't, and do you know why?"

"Because you're too lazy."

"No sir. The reason is that the last time me and you tried that, we had a little explosion."

Loper shrugged. "That was a freak. I'll have a look."

"Okay, buddy, you're paying the bills on this outfit."

Loper removed the air filter and looked into the carburetor. "Give 'er a crank." Sitting behind the wheel, Slim hit the starter and the motor turned over several times. It didn't start. Loper raised his hand in the air. "Hold it. I see the problem. It's getting too much gas."

Slim heaved a sigh and looked up at the sky. "Loper, the pickup's twenty years old and it wants to be traded off for a newer model. You can't run a ranch with junkyard equipment."

"Sure you can. That's how you stay in business in a bad cattle market." Loper walked into the barn and came back with a handful of wrenches. He flashed a grin. "I'll have it running in five minutes."

Slim shook his head. "In five minutes, you'll have parts strung out over three acres, and it still won't start."

Loper brought a finger to his lips. "Shhh.

You'll never learn anything if you're flapping your mouth all the time."

Loper leaned over the fender and went to work on the . . . whatever it was. Slim looked down at us dogs and grinned. "Y'all watch. He don't remember what happened the last time we tried this, but I do."

Slim drummed his fingers on the steering wheel while Loper clanked and banged under the hood. After about five minutes, he yelled, "Okay, give 'er a crank."

Slim stuck his head out the window. "Reckon you ought to step back a ways?"

Loper shook his head and rolled his eyes. "Slim, we're burning daylight."

"That ain't all we're fixing to burn."

"Crank the motor!"

"Okay, buddy, you asked for this."

Slim hit the starter and . . .

KA-BLOOEY!

The top half of Loper's body disappeared inside a cloud of blue smoke while his hat and several pieces of the former air filter floated down to the ground. As the smoke began to clear, I could see Loper standing there with a dazed expression on his face. He was still in one piece, but

it appeared that some of his hair had been singed and he'd lost about 30 percent of his mustache.

Slim was chuckling when he stepped out of the cab. "Are you hurt?"

"If I was, I wouldn't tell you about it." Loper snatched his hat off the ground and slapped it back on his head. "Find a nylon towrope and let's haul this wreck into town."

"You going to trade it off, finally?"

"No, I'm going to get it fixed. That's a good pickup."

"Oh yeah, when it ain't dead or blowing up. Loper, that thing's got two hundred thousand miles on it."

"That's right, and we'll drive it another two hundred thousand. Let's head for town."

"Loper?" Slim walked over and laid a hand on Loper's shoulder. "As one of the few friends you have left in this world, I need to tell you something." Loper shot him a suspicious glare. Slim leaned closer and whispered, "Half your mustache got blowed off. Before we go to town, you might want to trim the other side so you don't look like a crazy person."

Loper's hand went to his upper lip and felt around. He seemed surprised that Slim was right. "Get the towrope," he snarled, and went down to the house to trim his whiskers.

Well, that had started the morning off with a bang. (A little humor there. Did you get it? Started the morning off with a *bang*. Ha ha.) But when the cowboys left the scene of the explosion, I glanced around and realized that . . . Drover was missing! Fearing the worst, I searched the immediate area around the pickup and found no trace of the little mutt. What I found was . . .

I'm not sure that I should reveal this next part. I mean, all my training in Security Work had prepared me for the tragic side of life, but I'm thinking of the kids. You know my Position on Kids: I hate to scare 'em or shock 'em too badly, or give 'em stories that'll make 'em cry. And when I saw those little pieces of white fuzz on the ground . . .

Oops. I wasn't going to say anything but it just popped out, so now the cat is out of the sandbag. Okay, we might as well plunge into it.

In the course of conducting an All Points Search for Little Drover, who was missing in action, I found several fragments of whitish fuzz lying on the ground. They looked very much like . . .

I can't say it. It's too hard, too sad. I mean, Drover was the weirdest little met I'd ever mutted, but we'd worked together for years, and after all we'd been through together . . . a guy gets attached to his comrades, you know. We shouldn't. In a dangerous business like Security Work, we're always aware that, well, one of us might not come back from a haderous mission.

A hadderzous mission.

A hazzzeruss mission.

A hazzarduss mission.

HOW DO YOU SPELL THE STUPID WORD? I don't care. Skip it.

Now I don't remember what I was talking about. This really burns me up, because I know it was something important. The weather? Maybe that was it. The weather that morning was pretty nice, a little chilly but . . .

We weren't talking about the weather. Bones? Maybe so. I love bones, all kinds of bones, but I guess my favorite is steak bones. Ham bones are pretty nice, especially when they've been cooked in a big pot of pinto beans, but for flavor and chewing excitement, you can't beat . . .

Wait. Drover had vanished, remember? And we had just discovered a few pitiful fragments of his . . . well, his exploded body. I hate to put it that way (the kids), but sometimes we can't escape life's terrible tragedies, no matter how hard we try.

21

I heard a voice beside me. It said, "Boy, the air filter sure got shredded."

"That's not an air filter, pal. You're looking at the remains of a friend of mine."

"Gosh, how sad. What was his name?"

"His name was . . ." I turned and looked at the mysterious stranger who had . . .

HUH?

Never mind. Skip it. Sorry I brought it up.

CHAPTER THREE

Drover Wasn't Blown Up

You remember all that business about Drover's tragic death in an explosion? Ha ha. Just a small error, no big deal, a tiny malfunction in some of our, uh, equipment. I was misquoted, see. I had reported finding small shreds of whitish fuzz, but by the time the story got out, it had been blown completely out of . . .

Okay, here's the deal. You'll be shocked and surprised, so grab something solid and hang on. Drover didn't get blown up, exploded, vaporized, or rendered into doggie hamburger. Do you know why? Because at the first sign of trouble, *he slipped away and hid in the machine shed.*

I should have known. He does this all the time. He's such an incredible weenie. I don't know why I waste time worrying about him. The explosion has never been made that could move fast enough to catch Drover.

So there it is, and by now maybe you've figured out that the so-called Mysterious Stranger was actually Mister Slinkaway. How do you suppose that made me feel? It made me feel like an idiot. There I was, standing over his shattered remains and actually feeling sad about it . . .

Never mind. Our best course of action here is to forget the whole shabby affair and pretend that it never happened. In fact, it never happened. Honest. It was just a frigment of our imaginations.

There, we've got that out of the way.

Where were we? Oh yes, the pickup. Slim banged and clanged around in the machine shed until he found the big nylon towrope. He dragged it outside and hooked one end to the bumper of the broken pickup. He collected what was left of the air filter, pitched it on top of the motor, and slammed down the hood. By that time, Loper had returned from the house, and I noticed right away that he had done some snipping on his mustache.

Slim noticed too. A little grin tugged at his mouth as he watched Loper coming up the hill. "I think you're walking straighter now, with all that weight off the left side." Loper wasn't smiling. "Well, I tried to warn you."

"If we did it a thousand times, it would never happen again."

"Loper, if we did it a thousand times, there wouldn't be anything left of you but bones and a couple of pieces of meat. You're just too much of a donkey to admit the truth."

Loper walked up to him and glared into his eyes. "Am I going to hear about this for the rest of the day?"

"Well, I know all the mechanics in town would love to hear about you starting a pickup the Cowboy Way." Slim snorted a laugh.

"Slim, how would you like to spend the winter digging sewer lines in the snow?"

There was a long silence. Slim's smile faded. "As I was saying, my lips are sealed."

Loper drove his pickup around to the machine shed and they hooked the two pickups together with the towrope. Loper climbed into the lead pickup and Slim headed for the broken one. By the time his hand touched the door handle, Drover and I were right there, poised and ready to spring up into the cab.

See, we'd held a little conference and had

decided that, well, it had been a long time since we'd been to town. And we probably needed to go. Or, to frame it up from a different angle, we knew that Slim would *want* us to go. I mean, who'd want to make a long, lonely trip into town without a couple of crackerjack cowdogs?

He noticed us standing there, poised and quivering with excitement—the excitement that any normal, healthy American dog would feel at the prospect of going to the Big City.

Slim gave us a sour look. "What's this? You think you deserve to go to town?"

Well . . . yes, sure. Definitely. I mean, we had suffered with him through the Pickup Crisis, right?

"Okay, I'll let you go, but you'd better behave yourselves."

Oh, sure. No problem there. We would be Perfect Dogs, no kidding.

When he opened the door, I sprang upward with a mighty surge and . . . BONK . . . hit the steering wheel, you might say, and tumbled backward to the ground. But I leaped to my feet and tried it again, and made a smooth landing on the seat, and you'll notice that I got there several seconds ahead of Drover. Heh heh. That assured

me of getting my favorite spot in the pickup, the Shotgun Position beside the window on the passenger side.

When we were all settled inside the pickup, Slim slammed the door and let his gaze drift over to me. "Did you hit the steering wheel?"

Well, I . . . yes, maybe I did, but was that a big deal? I mean, any dog could have . . .

"Heh. You've got to watch out for those steering wheels, pooch. They'll jump right out in front of you."

Very funny.

Loper took the slack out of the towrope and we began our slow trip into town. An hour after leaving the ranch, we were driving down the main street of Twitchell, Texas. Wow, what an exciting place! It had everything: cars, people, stores. We passed Waterhole 83, the Dixie Dog Drive-in, Stockman's Western Wear, two gas stations, the picture show, and a grocery store.

We made a left turn at the stoplight and pulled up in front of Hergert Ford. There, Loper and Slim got out of their respective pickups and went inside to talk to the service manager. Before he left, Slim leaned inside the window and said, "Y'all stay here and be nice. We won't be long."

Yes sir! Being nice would be no problem at all. We were just thrilled to be in a huge city like Twitchell, even if we had to stay inside the pickup. What more could a couple of dogs from the country possibly . . .

Just then, a small red pickup pulled into a parking spot nearby. A man stepped out, reached into the bed of the pickup, and brought out a cardboard box. The lettering on the side of the box said TREJO'S DONUT DELIGHTS. He carried the box into the shop and closed the door behind him.

I thought nothing of this at the time, but several minutes later, my noseatory equipment began picking up signals of something . . . hmmm . . . good. Sweet. I gave the air a more thorough sniffing, and by George, the more I sniffed, the more I wanted to find out exactly where that smell was coming from.

I turned to my assistant, who was staring off into deep space. "Drover, may I interrupt for a second?" No response. "Drover? Hello? Is anyone home?"

At last his gaze drifted down and he gave me a silly grin. "Oh, hi. Are you back already?"

"I didn't go anywhere."

"Did you see anything exciting?"

"I didn't go anywhere. I've been sitting right here beside you."

"I'll be derned. I thought somebody got out and went somewhere."

"That was Slim."

"Oh yeah, now I remember. Sometimes I get bored and my mind wanders."

"No kidding? Drover, I need to ask you a question. Do you smell anything unusual?"

He sniffed the air. "Well, let's see. Dirty socks?"

"No. That's just the normal smell of Slim's pickup. Try again."

He sniffed. "Oh yeah, I smell it now. Two dogs. Maybe it's us."

I struggled for patience. "Drover, please try to be serious. Take a deeper sniff and try to analyze the various odors in the air."

He drew in a big sniff of air. His eyes popped wide open. "Oh my gosh, there it is!" He darted over to the window, stuck his nose outside, and sniffed some more. "I think it's coming from that red pickup. And it smells yummy."

"Exactly. Now we have two snifferations that point to something sweet and yummy. The question now is, what could it be?"

30

"Yeah. I wonder what it could be."

"That's what I just said. At this point, we don't have any reliable data on that."

He squinted at the lettering on the door of the red pickup. "Trejo's Do-nut De-lights. Gosh, I wonder what that means?"

I joined him at the window. "The same message was written on a box the man took inside. Hmm, this is very strange."

Drover leaned forward and widened his eyes. "Yeah, and you know what? There's a whole bunch of those boxes in the back of the pickup."

I took a closer look. "You're right, Drover, nice work."

"Thanks."

"It appears that we've stumbled upon boxes and boxes of donuts. The question that faces us now is . . . *what is a donut?*"

At that very moment, I notice a little gray poodle sitting in the seat of the pickup, with his eyes fixed on the door through which his master had gone. Drover saw him too. "Oh, look, there's a dog. Maybe he can tell us what a donut is."

Little did we know or suspect . . . well, you'll see.

CHAPTER FOUR

We Meet a Mouthy Little Yip-Yip

Have we discussed poodles? Maybe not. I've never had any use for 'em. They belong to the Yip-Yip branch of the dog family, don't you know, and there's no good that can come from a Yip-Yip.

See, your poodles tend to be spoiled, pampered, and mouthy, and this little shrimp appeared to follow the pattern all the way down the line. He had gray curls all over his body. He'd been clipped and shampooed, wore a rhinestone collar around his neck, had a red bow tied into the curls on his forehead and a ridiculous stump of a tail with a little hair puff on the end.

On a normal day, I wouldn't have bothered even to say hello to a poodle, much less tried to carry on a conversation with one, but Drover had raised a good point. We had discovered a cloud of interesting smells coming from that pickup and the evidence was beginning to suggest that the smells had something to do with *donuts*.

Since the yip-yip was sitting inside a pickup that appeared to be a donut-delivery vehicle, we had reason to suppose that he might provide us with important information.

Don't get me wrong. Our motives here were purely scientific. No kidding. We were just a couple of dogs with active minds, who hungered, so to speak, for knowledge about . . . well, Life and the universe and the wonders of . . . sniff, sniff . . . nature.

Like astronomers who look at the stars night after night, we were driven by an unquitchable desire to unlock the secrets of the universe and to expand . . . sniff, sniff . . . the frontiers of so forth.

See, for years and years, dogs all over the world had lived in the Dungeon of Ignorance, crying out in anguished voices, "What, oh what, is a donut?" And here we were, on the verge of the edge of the brink of making that very discovery.

We were filled with the excitement of . . . sniff, sniff . . . discovery. Oh yes! Our eyes sparkled with the pure clean light of curiosity. Our hearts sang noble choruses and our mouths watered with . . .

Never mind what our mouths were doing. You get the point. Our motives were as pure as the driveled snow and we had no interest, almost no interest whatever, in . . . well, food or eating or such low-life pursuits.

Honest. No kidding. It's very important that you believe this, because . . . well, you'll see.

Anyway, it was very clear what we had to do. As soldiers in the Battle for Knowledge, we had to pursue our research, no matter the risk or the cost, and if that meant that we had to speak to a poodle, well, it had to be done.

I gave Drover the signal that I would take the lead in this deal, and I opened things up by addressing the yip-yip in a pleasant tone of voice. "Hello over there. Yoo-hoo? You in the little red pickup? Hello." He came to the window and looked at us. I continued. "Hi there. We're visiting from the country and, well, wanted to meet some new friends. My name is Hank the Cowdog, and this is Drover, my assistant."

Drover grinned and wiggled his stub tail. "Oh, hi. We were just wondering what's in those—"

I cut him off just in time. "Shhh. Do you want him to get suspicious? I'll handle this." I turned a charming smile toward the mutt . . . toward the poodle, that is. "What's your name?"

In a squeaky little voice, he said, "Bear."

"Bear!" I burst out laughing.

"Something funny about that?"

"*Flea* would be closer to the truth. I mean, you're just a poodle, right?"

"What makes you think so?"

"Well, you know, the curls, the rhinestone collar, the bow in your hair. And you're kind of a shrimp."

"You got something against little guys?"

"Not especially. You're a peewee, that's all I'm saying."

He gave me a curled lip. "Check it out, buster. I'm not a poodle."

Drover and I exchanged glances, then Drover said, "Well, what are you?"

The mutt hopped his front legs up on the window ledge. "I'm a rottweiler."

After a moment of startled silence, I managed to say, "No kidding. A rottweiler, huh?"

"That's right, and you know what that means?"

"Uh . . . no. What does it mean?"

"It means"—he leaned toward us—"that you guys better stay away from my donuts. I saw you staring at 'em."

"Actually, pal, we're not even sure what

donuts are. Maybe you can tell us."

"Sweet pastries. They're great. Dogs love 'em, but you can't have any. Hee hee hee."

"Oh yeah? What makes you so sure about that?"

He tapped himself on the chest. "I do security for Trejo's Donut Delights."

I snorted a laugh. "Really! You're guarding a load of pastries?"

"Yeah. Fifteen dozen. Is that funny?"

I burst out laughing. "I'm sorry, pal, but yes, that's the funniest thing I've heard since you said you were a rottweiler."

He held his head at a haughty angle. "Oh yeah? Well, check this out, country boy. Two months ago, I sent two cowdogs and one collie to the hospital. Last week, I karate-chopped a boxer dog in two. Yesterday morning, I whipped, and we're talking *mauled,* a couple of Great Danes. They were trying to mess with Tom Trejo's donuts. When the ambulance came to pick 'em up, nobody was laughing."

"Oh yeah? Well, hear this: ha, ha, ha, ha! What do you think of that, huh?"

The little mutt shrugged. "I think you're dumb, like all the others. Dumb dogs always laugh. Then they *die* laughing."

I winked at Drover. "Wooooo! Hey, this is getting better and better. You know, for a pip-squeak, you sure talk a lot of trash."

"Yeah, but I back it up, dude. You don't believe me? Jump out that window. I dare you."

HUH? I took a closer look at him. "Maybe I didn't hear you right. Did you just *dare* me to jump out the window?"

"Yeah."

"This window right here?"

"Yeah."

"Just jump out on the ground, is that what you're saying?"

"Yeah, and let's make it a Double-Dog Dare."

Behind me, I heard Drover say, "Git 'im, Hankie, git 'im!"

My goodness, it appeared that events were rushing us toward a confrontation. I squared my enormous shoulders and gave the shrimp a look of purest steel. "Okay, pal, now you've done it. You should never challenge a ranch dog unless you're ready to face the consequences. Drover, hop down there and let's get this over with."

Drover gasped and shrank back. "Me! Are you crazy?"

We moved away from the window so that we could conduct our business in private. "What's

the problem? He's bluffing. He's just a little shrimp with a big mouth."

"If he's such a shrimp, how come he's guarding fifteen thousand donuts?"

"It's only fifteen dozen."

"Yeah, but he said he cut a dog in half with a karate chop!"

"So what? It's cheap talk. Drover, I'm thinking of your career. This would give you a chance to advance up the ladder of success. It's a great opportunity."

"Yeah, but you know this old leg of mine. It's killing me."

"Oh, brother. Drover, you're behaving like a selfish, chickenhearted little creep. I'm ashamed of you."

"Me too, so why don't you do it?"

"Huh? Well, I . . ." I studied Bear through the windshield. "He looks very confident, doesn't he?"

"Yeah. It makes me wonder. Maybe he really is a rottweiler."

"Don't be ridiculous."

"A miniature rottweiler."

"Hmm. I hadn't thought of that."

Drover was trembling now. "I've heard about those guys. They're double tough. Triple tough."

My mind was racing. "Drover, something very

strange is going on here, and it all boils down to one crucial question: Do we dare risk the Head of Ranch Security over something as trivial as a dare and a donut?"

"Heck yes. I'm starved."

"What?"

"I said, heck no."

"I agree. Until we can gather more information on this situation, we have no choice but to follow the . . . uh . . . Path of Maturity."

"You mean . . ."

"Exactly. We're going to sit this one out. We just can't risk it."

It was tough, let me tell you. In order to follow the Path of Maturity, we had to sit there and listen to that mouthy little . . . whatever he was . . . as he strutted back and forth, yelling, "We're number one! We're number one!" He gave us monkey ears, crossed his eyes, and even stuck out his tongue at us. He laughed, he sneered, he mocked us, he taunted us, he called us chickens and cowards and yellow-bellied country bumpkins.

And we had to sit there and take it. The entire Security Division was plunged into gloom. Never had we sunk so low. But then . . .

CHAPTER FIVE

The Donut Fiasco

The shop door opened and out walked the owner of the red pickup—Tom Trejo. He was no longer carrying the box of donuts, so I took this to mean that he had delivered them to the mechanics in the shop and was ready to leave.

On that small point, I happened to be wrong. Instead of climbing into the pickup, he walked up to the window and said (this is a direct quote), he said, "Hi, Poodzie. You doing okay?"

Drover and I exchanged glances of astonishment. POODZIE? The twerp had given us a phony name and was operating under a false identity! His name wasn't Bear and he was no more rottweiler than I was.

Then the little fraud flew into Tom's arms,

41

licked his face, and yipped with joy—exactly the sort of behavior you'd expect from a sniveling poodle. Then Tom said, "I'm talking with some of the boys. I'll be a while." His dark eyes moved to us. "Are those dogs bothering you?" Tom came lumbering over to our pickup, rested his elbows on the window ledge, and leaned inside. "Don't be messing with my poodle. He's got the sniffles." He lowered his voice to a growl. "And don't even *think* about getting into my donuts."

Yes sir.

He turned on his heel, blew a kiss to Poodzie, and disappeared inside the building. The instant we heard the door shut behind him, Drover and I gave each other a nod, rose to our respective feet (he rose to his, I rose to mine), and swaggered over to the open window. Poodzie Poodle was admiring his toenails.

"Poodzie, huh? That's a long way from Bear."

He curled his lip. "So? I can call myself anything I want."

"Yeah, well, I've got another name for you: Catfish Bait."

Behind me, I heard Drover giggle. "Oh, good shot!"

Poodzie–Catfish Bait made a sour face.

"You're so crude, I'm not even going to talk to you." He looked the other way.

"Ouch! Boy, that really hurt, Poodzie, but we need to talk."

"Go away."

"About that Double-Dog Dare you threw down a while ago? I think I'll take you up on it."

His head snapped around and he stared at me with wide eyes. "Don't you . . . I'm a black belt in Dog Karate, I'm not kidding."

I gave Drover a wink and hopped out the window. When my feet hit the ground, I could hear a gust of air rushing into the poodle's lungs. He squeaked, "Oh, you're going to get it now, you're really going to get it!" I took a step toward him. "Okay, one more step, dude!" I took one more step. "You're asking for it!" I took another step, and this time he let out a scream. "Help! Murder! He's going to hurt me!"

He vanished inside the cab of the pickup. I flashed Drover a wink, swaggered over to the red pickup, and hopped my front paws up on the window ledge. Inside, I could see Poodzie pressed against the door, quivering and moaning.

"Hey, Poodzie, didn't you say you had some fresh donuts in the back?"

He let out another screech. "Go away! Tom, help! There's five of 'em, they're beating me up! Help!"

"Well, I want you to pay close attention, son, because we're fixing to eat your donuts, every one of 'em."

"Don't you dare! Tom!"

I headed for the back of the red pickup. As I was passing the window of our pickup, I saw that Drover was enjoying the show. "Okay, son, it's time for us to go to work. We've got fifteen dozen donuts to eat, and not much time."

"You mean . . . "

"I mean you said you were starving, so let's eat."

His grin faded. "You know . . . I'm not as hungry as I thought. You go ahead."

"Fine, whatever you think. You'll be sorry, of course."

I marched around to the rear of Poodzie's pickup, went into the Deep Crouch Formation, and flew over the end gate as gracefully as a . . .

SMUSH!

. . . deer, but landed right in the middle of stack of boxes, sending them clattering in all directions and releasing a powerful cloud of . . . sniff, sniff . . . WOW! Holy smokes, you talk about

44

a great smell. One donut smells wonderful, but fifteen dozen . . . and I mean they were scattered all across the bed of the pickup!

The circuits in my Nosetory Scanners just melted. I hardly knew where to begin, so I just . . . well, snagged the nearest donut and wolfed it down.

Oh, mercy me! Oh, donut delight! They were as soft as a cloud, as sweet as a dream. Hey, Tom Trejo was more than a good cook. He was an artist with dough! This was Doggie Paradise! I wolfed and chewed and swallowed, wolfed and chewed and swallowed.

See, I knew we were on a time clock, so to speak, and I wanted to . . . a door opening? Footsteps? It didn't matter, I didn't care what happened. Let 'em send me to prison, let 'em shoot me! Whatever they did, I would go out a happy dog.

"Hank!"

Hey, don't bother me now, I've still got ten dozen left!

"HANK!"

Suddenly I felt myself . . . well, skidding backward, you might say, almost as though some mysterious force were pulling me by the . . . someone was pulling me by the tail! Pulling me away from

my precious cargo of golden puffy . . . I could hear my claws scraping across the bed of the pickup.

No, no, don't do this to me!

Next thing I knew, I was locked in the rough embrace of . . . someone . . . an angry scarecrow in cowboy clothes . . . okay, it was Slim. And he looked . . . uh . . .

"Hank, what in the cat hair are you doing!"

Well, I . . . there were fifteen boxes of donuts, see, and they smelled so wonderful . . . and nobody was guarding them . . . okay, a pipsqueak poodle, but for the most part, they were . . . uh . . . all alone back there, and I just thought . . .

Oh, brother. I reached toward the control panel of my mind and started throwing switches: Looks of Remorse; Mournful Wags on the tail section; Eyes of Tragedy. And then, to beef up the presentation, I switched on a little program we call "I Didn't Do It, Honest." I beamed them all toward Slim's . . . yipes . . . wrathful face.

The fog in my mind began to clear. I saw people. Tom Trejo was counting donuts and writing on a piece of paper. Loper stood a short distance away, looking toward the sky and shaking his head. Several mechanics had come outside and were laughing.

Slim wasn't laughing. "Hank, you birdbrain, get in the pickup! Now!"

Sure. Fine. No problem. But if he would just give me a minute, I could explain . . . he opened the pickup door and booted me in the tail.

"Get in there!"

I flew into the seat, which was no small deal, since I was stuffed to the gills and had taken on some extra weight.

Drover whispered, "Did you get in trouble?"

"Roger that."

"How bad?"

"Pretty bad, but I think it's fixing to get worse. The donut man is adding up the bill."

Slim and Loper were standing near Tom Trejo, watching in gloomy silence as he added up a long column of numbers. Loper said, "How much?"

"Oh," said Tom, "it's not as bad as I thought, only forty bucks. I'm giving you a volume discount."

Loper's eyes almost popped out of his head. "Forty bucks! Would you take the dog instead?"

Tom chuckled. "Nope, but we take checks."

Loper snatched the checkbook out of his hip pocket, bent over the hood of Trejo's pickup, and slashed off a check. His lips were white when he

48

handed it over. "Sorry about this. The dog is a moron, that's all I can say."

"It's okay, Loper. We're square." Trejo looked around and grinned. "Well, I guess he liked my donuts." No one laughed.

They shook hands. Slim and Loper went back inside the shop (giving me nullifying glares as they walked past) and Trejo got into his pickup and started the motor. And guess who made his appearance then: Poodzie Poodle. He flew into Tom's lap, leaped with joy, and licked him on the face. Tom laughed and rubbed the little snot behind the ears.

It was so disgusting, I had to turn away. But as Trejo was backing out of the parking space, I looked around, just in time to catch a glimpse of Poodzie Poodle. He was grinning and waving good-bye. Oh, and he yelled, "Thanks for the business, dude!"

I was so mad, I could have . . . never mind.

Just then, Slim and Loper came out of the shop, and we soon found out what had taken them so long. Loper had been arguing and pleading with the service manager to loan us another pickup until Slim's old wreck got fixed. Apparently he had won the argument.

Outside, Loper pitched the key to Slim and said, "See you back at the ranch, and don't get lost on the way. I hope your dog enjoyed his forty-dollar donuts."

"Don't blame me."

"You're the one who brought him to town."

"All right, we'll split the damages, fifty-fifty. You can take it out of my next paycheck. Will that make you happy?"

"Forget it. I'd rather pay the bill and complain about it."

Slim nodded. "Just what I figured. Where's this loaner pickup I'm supposed to drive?" Loper pointed to a shiny late-model red Ford parked next to ours. Slim let out a whistle. "That's awful fancy for our outfit. I won't know how to act, driving a pickup that works."

"Try not to tear it up. After paying for your dog's snack food, I'm broke." Loper walked to his pickup and drove off.

Drover and I were still sitting in the broken pickup. Slim came over to collect some of his personal things—gloves, fencing pliers, a shovel, and a log chain—and he was muttering under his breath. "I'll be hearing about them stinking donuts for the next six months. Thanks a bunch, Hank."

Me? Hey, had it ever occurred to him that we'd been *set up* on that donut deal? Of course not. When in doubt, blame Old Hank for everything that goes wrong. Well, for his information . . . burp, excuse me . . . for his information . . . boy, I was sure loaded up with . . . you know, donuts are delicious while you're eating them, but if you happen to gobble down a couple of boxfuls . . .

I wasn't feeling so great, and that's when I began to realize that donuts are cooked in GREASE. Had you thought of that? I hadn't. I mean, in the midst of the Donut Frenzy, I had thought they were as light and puffy as summer . . . bupp . . . clouds, but now . . . ooo, boy, I felt like I had two hundred pounds of cast iron in my stomach.

Bork. Mupp.

All at once it seemed hot and stuffy inside the pickup. I could hear my innards twisting and squeaking, as my poor body fought against the Grease Invasion. Stale grease. Yucko grease. Oily, oozey, slimy, gooey, greasy grease. Grease forever, grease everywhere!

Drover must have heard my stomach rumbling. His ears shot up and he stared at me. "Is that you?"

"Yes. I hate donuts."

"No fooling? How come you ate so many?"

"Drover, small minds always ask obvious . . . hick . . . questions."

"Sorry."

"Don't you get it? I lost my head, I got swept up in a frenzy of . . . *I've got to get out of here!*"

Slim was still loading stuff and the door on the driver's side hung open. I shoved past Drover, staggered across the seat, bumped into Slim, and made a dive for the sidewalk. I arrived there just in time, for my tormented body had already entered into the Anti-Grease Flush Program.

For the next thirty seconds, all circuits and systems moved out of my control. I mean, I knew this was a bad place to do it, right there on the sidewalk in front of the Ford dealership, but my entire body had been taken over by invisible forces and I had become a helpless bystander.

When the storm passed, so to speak, I felt much better, and dared to let my gaze wander over to Slim. His chin had slumped against his chest and his right hand covered his eyes. Shaking his head, he mumbled, "I hope nobody's watching this."

Well? What's a dog supposed to do, drown in grease?

Slim collected the rest of his stuff, pitched

Drover out of the cab, and slammed the door. "Come on, you clowns, let's sneak out of town before I get arrested."

Did he ask about my health? Did he care that I had repelled an attack of Deadly Donut Toxins? Oh no. All he could think about was . . . never mind.

We followed him to the loaner pickup and formed a line beside the driver's-side door. Loyal dogs to the end, we were ready to load up and take our usual spots on the seat, where we could keep Slim company and help him with the long drive back to the ranch.

He looked down at me and curled his lip. "You think you're going to ride in a nice pickup after that? Get in the back. That's the place for hogs and low-class mutts."

Hogs and low-class mutts? Fine. If that's the way he felt about it, I had no problem riding in the back. Furthermore, what made him think that I even *wanted* to ride up front with him? After all the hateful things he'd said, I wasn't sure I would EVER ride in the cab with him again.

It's sad when old friendships come to an end, but I knew that things would never be the same between us again. He had destroyed something precious inside me, trampled on the feelings of a dog who had devoted his whole life to pleasing his people.

We dogs rode back to the ranch in the bed of the pickup. When we pulled up in front of the machine shed, I jumped out and walked away.

It was over with us. Forty dollars' worth of greasy donuts had cost me one of the dearest friends of my life.

CHAPTER SIX

I Lost My Pal in a Pile of Dough

By this time, you probably have mist in your eyes and the pages of the book are beginning to blur. I understand. It almost broke my heart, leaving Slim forever. In fact, it was such an unspeakable tragedy that I sat down in the musty silence of the machine shed and composed a song of farewell. If it causes you to burst out crying . . . well, there's nothing we can do about that.

I Lost My Pal in a Pile of Dough
That scene in town was no big shucks.
They won't go broke for forty bucks.
And what occurred brought them no shame.
They've always got old Hank to blame.

Perhaps I could have shown restraint
And saved poor Slim from social taint.
But grease is deadly, that we know,
I lost my pal in a pile of dough.

I regret all the feelings this deal has
    evoked,
Resentment and anger my actions have
    stoked.
I guess he'd be happy if I had just
    croaked,
Expired from the grease in which I was
    soaked.

I never thought it would come to this.
Our friendship wasn't perfect bliss,
But true it was, or so I thought,
Now, it seems, it's come to naught.

I thought our bond could stand the test,
At times it seemed the very best.
But now it's gone, like melted snow.
I lost my pal in a pile of dough.

Okay, I was foolish for fooling around,
Plundering donuts and wolfing them
    down,

Then leaving them there in a pile on the
    ground,
Embarrassing Slim in the middle of town.

For years I've been his closest mate.
You'd think that he could tolerate
A fault or two . . . or even ten.
I thought he had a thicker skin.

It's sad, so sad, to contemplate
What might have been . . . but it's too late.
He had a friend but let me go.
I lost my pal in a pile of dough.

    But for crying out loud, nobody got hurt!
    It wasn't a crisis or national alert.
    We didn't have bodies or blood in the dirt.
    A dog merely happened to toss his dessert.
    A dog merely happened to toss his dessert!

Pretty sad song, huh? You bet. As I wrote
those painful words, tears were streaming down
both sides of my face, dripping off my chin, and
forming a Pool of Tragedy at my feet. No kidding,
composing that song was one of the toughest as-
signments of my whole career, but it was a job
that had to be done.

To be honest, I wasn't sure that I could go on. For all those years, Slim had been such an impointant park of my life . . . important part of my life, I just couldn't imagine that it had all come to an end. I mean, think about all the happy times we'd known: feeding cattle together in the snow, sharing the same bed on cold winter nights, splitting a mackerel sandwich in the shade of a cottonwood tree . . .

Actually, the mackerel sandwich brought back a few unpleasant memories, since it had given me incredible indigestion, but you get the point.

Slim and I had been as close as two peas in a pot, two toes on a foot, two feet in a boot, two boots on a porch, two porches on a house, two houses on a street. In me, he'd had a loyal friend who didn't care that he was nasty bachelor, and in him, I'd had . . . well, not much, it appeared, since he'd allowed our relationship to be destroyed over one measly incident in town.

Okay, I had to accept a tiny share of the blame. If I'd eaten two donuts instead of two hundred, maybe things would have turned out differently, but still . . .

Well, it was over now, years of friendship down the Toilet of Life. I would have to leave the ranch, of course, and become a homeless wanderer, but I was so distressed and broken up that I decided to postpone my departure until the following day. I spent a restless night on a bed of rags in a dark corner of the machine shed.

The next morning, just as I was preparing to leave, I heard someone calling my name. "Hank? Are you in there? Hank?"

It was Drover, of course, the last true friend I had in the world. That gives you some idea of how far I had fallen. I jacked myself up from the bed of rags and made my way to the big sliding doors. Sure enough, there he stood in morning's light, a simple, pea-brained little mutt who seemed delighted to see me.

When I appeared, he started hopping around in circles. "Oh good, I'm so happy! I worried about you all night. I thought maybe you'd . . . well, run away or something. You sure looked sad when we got back from town."

I slipped through the crack between the big sliding doors and stepped outside. "Thanks, Drover. I'm touched by your concern, but you probably shouldn't waste your time worrying about me."

"What do you mean?"

"It's obvious, isn't it? That incident in town pretty muchly sank my ship. It's all over between me and Slim."

He stopped jumping around and stared at me. "You mean, eating all those donuts?"

"Right. I don't know what came over me. If I'd just eaten a couple, it would have been no big deal, but was I satisfied with two or three? Heck no, I tried to eat the whole load! It was one of the dumbest stunts I've ever pulled."

"Yeah, but any dog would have done the same."

"Drover, any dog *wouldn't* have done the same. You didn't. You sat there in the pickup and watched the whole thing, and you didn't get in trouble. You never get in trouble. I don't know how you do that, but it really burns me up."

He grinned. "It's easy. I'm a chicken."

I studied the runt for a long moment. "You're admitting that you're a chicken?"

"Oh, sure. You would have found out sooner or later."

I wasn't in a laughing mood, but that made me laugh. "Uh . . . Drover, it's pretty obvious."

"It is?"

"Of course it is. You'd have to be blind and deaf not to notice."

"Darn." His head drooped. "I wanted to keep it a secret. See, I hate being such a chicken."

"Well, it seems to be working, pal. You've still got a job and I'm living under a cloud of shame and disgrace. An outside observer might say that you've got the better end of the deal."

"Yeah, but it's so boring. Sometimes I wish I could be more like you, daring and bold."

"That's me all right, daring and bold. Also homeless and out of a job."

He let out a gasp. "Gosh, you mean . . ."

"I have no choice, Drover. After yesterday . . ." Just then, we heard the sound of an approaching vehicle. My first instinct was to go straight into the Alert and Alarm Procedure, but then I remembered: it wasn't my job anymore. "Yes, Drover, I'm leaving the ranch."

"That's Slim's pickup. He's coming this way."

"Well, that gives me all the more reason to hit the road. I'm sure he won't want to see me hanging around."

I started to leave, but Drover darted after me. "No, wait. Give him a chance, see what he says. Maybe . . . Hank, I don't think he'd want you to leave."

I stopped. "Really?"

"Yeah, and if you look sad and sorry, maybe he'll forget about it."

I gave that some thought. "Hmmm. Well, I've got nothing to lose. I could try the Deepest Remorse Program."

"Yeah, it's worked before, and I'll help. We'll both look sad and sorry."

I laid a paw on his shoulder. "Tell you what, let's give it a shot. If it works, there just might be a promotion waiting for you."

"Oh, goodie, a promotion. I can hardly wait."

We hustled back to the machine-shed doors. "Okay, soldier, you set up here, and I'll set up over there. We'll need to be in position when he pulls up, and be ready to roll tape the very instant his foot touches the ground. And remember, Drover, what we're selling here is Funeral."

"Funeral. Got it. Here I go!"

He sprinted over to his position on the west side of the sliding doors and I took up mine on the east side. When Slim arrived, there would be no way he could avoid seeing our presentation.

I heard the crunch of his tires on the gravel drive and hurried through my Looks of Deepest Remorse checklist: Dead Tail, Lifeless Ears, Drooped Head, Hollow Eyes, and Dispirited Lips. By the time Slim pulled up in front of the shed, I had everything set and ready. I shot a glance at

Drover and was pleased to see that he was in position too.

The stage was set. This would be one of the most important presentations of my whole career. If we could pull it off, maybe my life would return to its normal state. If we failed . . . I didn't even want to think about it.

Are you feeling the tension? I was. It was so thick, you could have cut it with a spoon.

The pickup stopped. A door opened. Slim's left foot touched the ground, then his right foot. The pickup door slammed. Moving at his usual pace (cold molasses), he walked toward the sliding doors, only . . . hey, what was the deal? He was looking at the ground, not at us, and . . .

I couldn't believe it. He walked right past us and went inside. He didn't even see us!

I shot a glance at Drover. He was looking discouraged. "Be brave, son, and try to stay on task. He'll be back in a second and we'll get another shot."

"Okay, I'll try to keep my spirits up."

"No, no, keep your spirits down. Don't forget: Funeral."

"Oh yeah, got it."

We heard Slim rummaging around for something on the workbench. Then . . . footsteps coming our way again. He stepped outside. I went to full power on the Remorse Transmitter. He walked toward the pickup . . . and his eyes were still on the ground.

He still hadn't seen us! What did it take to get this guy's attention?

He reached for the door handle. Okay, we were out of time. I had no choice but to go into Moans and Wails. I filled my lungs with air and unleashed a mournful groan that froze him in his tracks.

"Ah-oooooooo-roooor!"

Slowly, his head twisted around. He saw Drover. Then his gaze drifted over to me. His eyebrows lowered. "What's going on around here? Y'all look like you just came back from a funeral."

It was working!

He walked over to me and gave me a closer inspection. "You sick?"

Uh . . . no, not sick. That was yesterday. Today . . . distressed. Sorrowful. Overwhelmed by regrets and remorse. And feelings of guilt, terrible guilt.

He scratched the back of his neck. "Well, you ought to be sick, after what you done."

I rolled my eyes upward and went to Slow Taps on the last two inches of my tail.

"Are you sorry you made a pig of yourself?"

Oh yes, deeply sorry.

"Are you sorry you barfed on the sidewalk?"

Absolutely. I'd hardly slept a wink. The guilt and remorse had just eaten me alive. No kidding.

He knelt down on one knee and laid a hand on top of my head. "Being a dumbbell sure hurts, don't it?"

Oh yes, definitely, although . . . well, I don't know as I would have put it that way.

"It happens that I have some personal experience with that myself, which is why I have trouble staying mad at you, pooch. You remind me so much of me."

Oh, really? Well, I . . . I hardly knew what to say.

He aimed a finger at the end of my nose. "If I let you clowns go feed cattle this morning, reckon you could act halfway civilized?"

Oh yes, no question. Halfway or even two-thirds. Absolutely. Yes.

He pressed his lips together in a tight line and narrowed his eyes. "Okay, let's load up. Maybe we'll see my pet coyote today."

I hardly noticed his mention of the so-called pet coyote. All that mattered right then was that

I had saved my job! Slim and I were pals again, oh, happy day!

I couldn't contain myself. I leaped into his loving embrace, only . . . well, he didn't give me a loving embrace because I more or less knocked him backward, and while he was sprawled on the ground I licked his face from ear to ear. He laughed and grabbed me around the middle, and for several moments we wrestled and rolled around on the ground. Hey, it was just like old times. I'd gotten my life back and . . .

HUH?

Slim froze. I froze. Somebody was . . . standing over us.

CHAPTER SEVEN

We Ride in the Fancy New Pickup

My eyes moved up the stranger's legs and came to rest on . . . Loper's face. He was standing on one leg and sucking breakfast particles out of his teeth.

"Am I interrupting something?"

Slim grabbed his hat off the ground and pushed himself up to his feet. "Oh no, me and Hank was just . . . rassling."

"Rassling."

"Playing around."

"Oh. Well, I just wondered if there was a chance you might feed cattle this morning. 'Course, we could put it off for a few days, if it's not convenient."

Slim gave him a scowl. "You just love catching me in awkward moments, don't you?"

Loper snorted a laugh. "I do, I really do. Thanks, Slimbo, you've made my whole day." He started walking away, but when his eyes fell on me, his smile fell like a dead pigeon. "Forty bucks." Shaking his head, he walked down to the corrals.

Well, gee, did we have to bring up ancient history? Hey, we'd already worked through that crisis and had moved on with our lives.

Oh well. Slim and I had made peace and he'd invited us to help him on his feed run. And you know what else? He even let us ride in the cab of that fancy new loaner pickup! No kidding. I could hardly believe it, after the fuss he'd made about the Donut Fiasco. But that was the nice thing about Slim. He didn't hold a grudge. He didn't hang on to his anger the way some people did. (I won't mention any names.)

Yes I will. Loper.

Once we were settled inside the cab of the new pickup, Slim started the engine and listened to it for a second. "It's a diesel. What do you think?"

Well, it was . . . loud. Real loud. Sounded like a dump truck.

"I like the sound of a diesel. And check this

out." He snapped on the radio. "It works, and so do the windshield wipers." He turned on the wipers and grinned like a little boy. "Oh, and look at this." He pushed a button on the armrest and . . . amazing. The window on the passenger side zipped up. He gave us a wink. "Heh. Electric winders. And it's even got electric door locks." He pushed another button on the armrest, causing the door-lock gizmos to move up and down. "What do you think of that?"

Incredible. Drover and I were speechless. We had never known such luxury, or even imagined it.

"This pickup's way too fancy for me, but I won't mind being pampered for a few days. Heck, I deserve it, after all those years of driving Loper's junk heaps. Don't you dogs agree?"

Oh yes, no question about it. He deserved to be pampered . . . and, well, so did we. After all, we had put up with those junk-heap pickups too— the bad smells, the dust, the rough rides over pasture roads. I'd never been the kind of dog who craved luxury or pampering (it'll make a poodle out of you if you're not careful), but I figured that I could stand a couple of days of it.

Slim stepped on the clutch and shifted up into first gear, and we drove around to the stack lot to load up some hay. That winter, we were feeding cake (cubed feed in sacks) to most of the cows, but feeding hay to one bunch of cows that had baby calves. Why hay? Well, as I recall, it had something to do with . . . what was it? Milk production, there we go. Alfalfa hay, it seems, is a good type of feed for cows that are nursing calves. It helps them produce more milk . . . or something like that.

Slim did most of the work of loading the bales onto the bed of the pickup. Okay, he did *all* the work. Ranch dogs can do many things, some of them really amazing, but loading bales of hay isn't one of them. But that didn't mean that I sat around on my duff and loafed while Slim was working hard, loading the bales. No sir. Every time he lifted a bale, I was right there beside him, checking for . . .

"Hank, get out of the way."

. . . mice. See, when cold weather comes, your field mice leave the fields and pastures and . . .

"Hank, move!"

. . . take up residence in the cracks between the bales of hay. Once inside the stack, they'll dig holes in the hay, build nests, and generally make a mess of . . .

"HANK!"

Huh?

"I can't carry this bale of hay to the pickup when I'm stumbling over you."

Oh.

"Now get off the stack. Go sit on the ground and scratch a flea."

Sure, no problem.

Anyway, as I was saying, sometimes a dog's best course of action in these hay-loading situations is to sit on the ground, scratch a couple of fleas, and watch. But that's not the same as loafing. Loafing is an entirely different deal, and it's not something you'll ever catch ME doing. Now, Drover's a different story, but we don't need to go into that.

Slim loaded twenty bales onto the bed of the pickup and we set out for the northwest pasture. He rolled the windows down, which allowed me to stick my head outside. Dogs like to do that, you know. We like to hang our heads out the windows because . . . well, who wants to look out at the world through a piece of glass? Not me. I like to be involved, right in the middle of things.

Slim watched as I stuck my head out the window. "Hank, those electric buttons are on your side too, so be careful where you step."

Sure, no problem. You know, there's something really special about hanging your head out the window of a moving pickup. I'm speaking as a dog, of course. Humans don't seem to get as much of a kick out of it as we do.

For us, it's something really special. Did you know, for example, that if you hold your head at a certain angle, the wind will cause your ears to flap around? No kidding. And at another angle, if you let your tongue hang out the side of your mouth, the wind will cause the old tongue to flutter. I'm serious. And it's a pretty neat sensation.

Anyway, there's a little lesson on our Window Procedures, and it explains why I always choose to sit in the Shotgun Position, next to the window. I love the sensation of fresh air blowing across my face.

But wouldn't you know? Drover started whining about it. "Gosh, I wish I could ride Shotgun sometimes."

I pulled my head back inside and faced the runt. "What?"

"I said, you never let me ride Shotgun, so I never get to stick my head out the window."

"That's correct, and do you know why?"

"Because you're selfish?"

"No, just the opposite. I'm doing it for your own good. Drover, do you have any idea just how

74

dangerous it is to stick your face out the window of a moving pickup?"

"I guess not."

"It's very dangerous. Consider the facts. When you're moving along at thirty miles an hour, if a grasshopper happened to fly up and hit you in the face, why, there's no telling how much damage it might cause."

"I never thought about that."

"That's why I'm here, son, to protect you from hazards you're not aware of. Now, you take those big green grasshoppers. They can actually break off a tooth, damage your nose, or even knock out an eye."

"Oh my gosh. Knock out your eye?"

"No kidding. They'll knock it right out of your head. How would like that?"

"I wouldn't. This stub tail is bad enough."

"Well, there you are. You thought I was being selfish about the window? Well, now you know the truth." I laid a paw on his shoulder. "I'm only trying to protect you from a deadly Grasshopper Encounter."

"Gosh, thanks." He thought for a moment, then scowled. "Yeah, but we don't have grasshoppers in the wintertime. I haven't seen one in two months."

"Drover, the fact that you haven't seen any grasshoppers doesn't mean they're not still lurking around. It merely means you haven't seen one. They're very sneaky, you know."

"I didn't know that."

"They are. Very sneaky. Never trust a grasshopper. Just when you think they're all gone, one'll fly up from the ditch and knock your eye out. We just can't risk it."

He hung his head. "I guess you're right. But I get tired of breathing stale air all the time."

"Drover, stale air is better than no air at all. How would you like to live in a deep dark mine shaft, where there was no air?"

"I wouldn't like it. I'm scared of the dark."

"Well, there you are. Sitting in the middle of the seat, you get plenty of sunshine and stale air. You should count your blessings and stop complaining. Now, if you'll excuse me, I need to get back to my window."

I stuck my head out the window and feasted on a blast of clean, fresh air. WOW! Terrific. Over the roar of the wind, I heard Drover's voice. "Yeah, but how come the grasshoppers never knock out *your* eye?"

"I'm sorry, son, we're out of time for questions. Save it for another day."

Hanging my head out the window was great, one of the special joys of being a dog. It saddened me that Drover couldn't share the experience, but . . . well, there's only one Shotgun window on a pickup and one of us had to . . .

Huh?

All at once the window glass began sliding up. Shocked and alarmed, I backed away from it and barked. That seemed to work. The window stopped dead in its tracks . . . although windows don't exactly leave tracks. Anyway . . . no problem.

When we reached the northwest pasture, the cows were standing on the feed ground, waiting for us. Twenty or thirty of them, all standing around in small clusters. Cows have a pretty good sense of time, did you know that? They do, which is pretty amazing, considering that cows are really dumb about most things. Once we've established a pattern for the daily feed run, they expect us to be there at the same time every day, and if we're not, they'll stand there, mooing and complaining until we show up.

Slim stepped out of the pickup and counted the cows. They were all present. He got back inside and rigged the gearshift for Automatic Pilot, his usual feeding procedure. You might recall that when he fed hay by himself, he put the pickup in Grandma Low gear, let out on the clutch, and let the pickup drive itself, whilst he scrambled onto the bed on the pickup and tossed out the hay.

This was nothing new to me, I mean, Slim and I had done it many times before and it had always worked to perfection. Okay, not always. You might recall that he had once jumped out when the windows were rolled up, and had somehow managed to lock himself out of the pickup. That had been a pretty scary deal, since I had been left alone in a runaway pickup.

But Slim had learned from his careless mistake, and this time, he left both windows down so there was zero chance of it happening again.

He put the pickup in low gear and let out on the clutch. It started moving. He stepped out, climbed up into the back end, and started throwing off hay. Me? As you might expect, I took this opportunity to stick my head out the Shotgunside window and draw in more deep breaths of fresh . . .

Zzzzzzzzip.

Huh?

CHAPTER EIGHT

Trapped Alive!

My goodness, unless I was badly mistaken, the window glass had moved again. What was the deal? For no good reason, the glass had moved, with nobody cranking it up and without my permission.

No kidding. I stood there and watched as it zipped shut. You know, this was starting to get on my nerves. Not only had the window closed without any authorization from me, but it had denied me my source of fresh, wholesome air. But did I just sit there, moping and breathing stale air? No sir. I moved my freight over to the driver's-side window.

I stepped past Drover and headed for the open window. I suppose that his mind had been wandering and all at once it returned to his body. "What's going on? How come . . ."

"Don't worry about it, son. I've got everything under control." I stepped up to the window on the driver's side and filled my lungs with fresh air.

Behind me, Drover said, "Gosh, did the other window roll up by itself?"

"Something like that. Yes."

"Oh, I get it now. You stepped on the button."

"Button? I don't know what you're talking about."

"Well, there's a button . . ."

"There's a button on every shirtsleeve and a thread on every button, and I don't have time to discuss threads and buttons. The impoitant point is that we still have a supply of fresh air."

"Yeah, but you'd better watch where you're stepping or you'll do it again."

"Drover, where I'm stepping has nothing to do with . . ."

Zzzzzzzzzzzip.

HUH?

I happened to be looking at Drover at that very moment, and was able to observe his eyes as they grew from small dots into wide circles. Then he let out a gasp. "Oh my gosh, you rolled up that window too! I knew it! I tried to warn you!"

"Will you please hush? I had nothing to do with it. I was just standing here, minding my own business." My gaze prowled around the cab. "Drover, there's something very strange about this pickup. We must stay alert."

He fell down on the seat and started wheezing. "Yeah, and now I can't breathe!"

Of course you can breathe."

"Yeah, but all the air's gone stale, and I hate to breathe stale air. I think I'm fixing to smuthocate!"

"Oh, rubbish. Drover, it's common knowledge that these pickup cabs aren't sealed airtight. There should be plenty of . . ." I took a big gulp of air. All at once it seemed . . . uh . . . pretty stale. I took another big gulp and . . . "Holy stokes, Droper, we're running out of air!"

"I knew it! Help, I'm smuthocating!"

"Get control of yourself, son. We have to be professional about this. Try to . . ." My mind was racing. "Try to ration your air intake."

He stared at me. "How do you do that?"

"Well, you just . . . I'm not sure."

"Ohhhhhhh!"

"Stop groaning, that's the first step. Groaning

uses up large quantities of precious carbon diego. No more groaning."

"Well, I'll try. And maybe we should sit still and not move."

"Great idea. Now we're cooking." I left the window and joined him in the middle of the seat. There, we went into Statue Mode and didn't move a hair. The pickup chugged on across the pasture, Slim pitched off hay, and we rationed our breathing, cutting each breath by 46 percent. "I think this is working, son. Now, all we have to do is wait for Slim. What do you say? Can we tough it out?"

No answer. I glanced to my right and saw that he had passed out. A cold chill moved down my spine.

"Drover, speak to me. Can you hear me?"

He moaned. "What did you say?"

"Well, I haven't actually said anything yet, except, 'Speak to me.'"

"Do you want me to speak or hear you?"

"I don't care, one or the other."

"Well, I can't hear you. Everything's fuzzy."

"Okay, then speak to me."

"I just did."

"Yes, but you didn't say anything."

"Who can talk when he's smuthocating?"

"Try it, Drover, and give me a report on your condition."

"What? You're fading out."

"I said, give me a comport on your rendition!"

"Nothing makes sense, everything's fading out!"

"Hang on, son, don't lose consciousness. Slim's almost done, he'll be here any second."

"Everything's getting dark!"

"Open your eyes, Drover!"

He opened his eyes and blinked them several times. "That helped."

"See? Hang on for a few more minutes. Ration your air. Count sheep. Think of a letter between one and ten. Or . . . wait, we'll play Twenty Questions. That'll help pass the time."

"Who goes first?"

"You go. I'm feeling a little rattled."

"Okay, I'll try." He wadded up his face in an expression of deep concentration. "Here's my first question. How come you don't roll down a window?"

I stared at the runt. "Why don't I roll down the window? Because there's no crank or handle for doing it. Had you thought of that?"

"Yeah, but maybe if you go back to the door and step on one of those buttons . . ."

"Hold it, halt. We discontinued that conversation about threads and buttons."

"Yeah, but see those buttons on the door?"

I narrowed my eyes and studied the alleged door. "Oh. *Those* buttons? Okay, what's your point?"

"Well, I think if you step on one of them, it'll make the window roll down."

"Drover, that is one of the dumbest things you've ever said. How could a button roll down a window?"

He heaved a sigh. "Hank, just try it. I think it'll work."

I gave this half a minute of deep thought. "All right, I'll trust you this time. Everything in my experience tells me that this is a mistake, but for you, I'll try it."

"Thanks. You'll be glad."

I marched over to the left-side door, placed my paw on the button, and pushed down.

Click.

That was odd. The sound of a window moving up or down is supposed to be a *Zzzzzzzip*. The sound I'd just heard had been more of a *click*. Obviously Drover's experiment had ended in failure.

Behind me, I heard him let out a groan. "Oh no! YOU LOCKED THE DOORS!"

"I did no such thing. All I did was . . ." I looked closer at the little door-locker thing near the window. It appeared to be . . . gulp . . . in the *down* position. "Drover, I don't want to alarm you . . ."

"Help!"

". . . but something has gone badly wrong. This pickup has locked its own doors!"

"Help!"

"We are now locked inside a moving pickup!"

"Help!"

"Will you please shut your little trap and stop squeaking? I can't think with all your noise."

"Murff!"

"What?"

"I'm trying to gag myself."

"Oh. Thanks. Listen carefully. We have only one course of action left."

"Bust out?"

"No. We must *hide*. When Slim finds that the windows are rolled up and the doors are locked, he'll probably blame it on us."

"Gosh, I never thought of that."

"Quick, son, into Bunker Positions! Hit the floor!"

In a flash, we both dived out of the seat, hit the floor, and began burrowing as deeply as we could against the passenger-side door. To add to our concealment, we covered our eyes with our paws. We vanished into the darkness and became Invisible Dogs.

"Nice job, son, I think this will work."

"You really think so?"

"Oh yes. He'll never suspect a thing."

We hovered there in the darkness, listening to the drone of the motor. But then . . . oops, I heard Slim pulling on the door handle, trying to get inside. Then he was banging on the window glass. Then we heard his voice: "Hey!"

"Shhh. Not a peep, Drover. As long as he's outside, we're safe."

There was a long moment of silence. Then Drover said, "You know, I'm not so sure we're safe."

"What?"

"The pickup's still moving . . . and nobody's driving."

"Well, of course. What's your point, Drover, and please be quick about it."

"Well, I was just wondering if maybe . . . we ought to try to let him in."

"What? Are you nuts? If we let him in, he'll know we locked him out."

"*You* did, not me."

"Drover, I had nothing to do with it. On the

other hand . . ." I uncovered my eyes and sat up. I could see Slim's face in the window. He was yelling words I couldn't hear. "Drover, Slim's at the door. Maybe I'd better see what he wants."

I went to the door on the driver's side. Through the window, I could see Slim, trotting along beside the moving pickup. He yelled and banged on the window and pointed to something up ahead. Hmmm. A canyon. Then he pointed to the little door-locker device on the window ledge. What was he trying to tell me?

Bark? Okay, that made sense. He wanted me to bark. I filled my lungs with stale air and cut loose with a burst of deep, manly barking.

This produced a very strange response. His eyes seemed to roll up inside his head and he continued screaming and pounding on the window.

Bark louder? Sure, I could handle that. I refilled my tanks and unleashed an enormous barst of burking, one of the most impressive bursts of barking of my whole career. But even that didn't seem to help. I mean, he was still out there, yelling and waving like a lunatic.

What was he trying to say? Did he want me to start chewing on the steering wheel? Maybe that was it. I mean, sometimes in very stressful situation, a dog can make things better by, well,

chewing on something. I stepped up on the armrest to tell him that I'd gotten his message, but then . . .

Zzzzzzzzzip.

I'll be derned. The window rolled down. Amazing! Slim reached his hand inside, pulled up the locking device, jerked open the door, pushed me out of the way, threw himself into the seat, turned the key, and shut off the motor. The pickup chugged to a stop.

The atmosphere inside the cab became very . . . quiet, shall we say. Slim was panting and staring straight ahead with glazed eyes. He reached up a hand and removed his hat, then used it to fan his face. His hands were shaking.

Drover and I exchanged uneasy glances. The silence became very heavy as we wondered what would happen next. Thunder and lightning? Screams of anger? Accusations hurled at us from all directions? We waited in the deadly silence, our hearts pounding like beating hearts.

At last, Slim blinked his eyes and let out a big gust of air, then his gaze slid around to . . . uh . . . ME. I cringed and prepared myself for a blast.

I sensed that I was in trouble. But for what?

CHAPTER NINE

Drover Gets a Promotion

I had done nothing, but it appeared that I was in trouble again, and let's face the facts. This wasn't a great time for me to be in trouble. I mean, the Donut Fiasco had done some serious damage to my reputation and I'd gone to a lot of trouble to redeem myself—less than an hour ago. The timing here was bad, very bad.

I hung my head and waited for the storm to hit. To my amazement, it didn't come. Slim wasn't even mad! In a croaky voice, he said, "That canyon up yonder drops twenty feet straight down. If this new pickup had gone over the edge, Loper would have wrung my neck. Let's try not to do that again, what say?"

Whew! I could have hugged him. I hadn't done

anything in the first place, but I took a Pledge never to do it again.

With a shaky hand, he pushed a shock of hair back from his forehead. "I forgot about the electric winders. They ought to outlaw them things for ranch trucks."

Exactly. Windows that rolled themselves up, doors that locked for no reason. It was scandalous, shameful, outrageous. Slim and I were furious. This pickup was booby-trapped and not safe for innocent dogs.

When Slim had calmed down enough to start the pickup, we drove back to headquarters and loaded twenty sacks of feed onto the bed of the pickup. Then we headed east on the Wolf Creek Road to feed some more cattle. Slim seemed to be in a better mood now and so was I.

There was only one small dark cloud that blocked the sunshine in the clear sky of my horizon. The window on the Shotgun side was rolled up, see, and I wasn't able to do my Fresh Air Procedures. Maybe you think that's not a big deal, but for a ranch dog, it's a big deal. I needed some air.

But what's a dog to do? I had to sit there in the Shotgun position, looking out at the world through a sheet of glass and breathing stale air.

Have we discussed Air Quality? Studies have shown that dogs who breathe stale air for long periods of time become . . . well, stale. Dull-minded. Lazy. Legargic. I mean, look at what stale air had done to Drover.

I definitely needed some fresh air, and that's when I noticed that the window on Slim's side was rolled down. Would he mind if I . . . well, eased over to his side and shared the window with him? Maybe he wouldn't notice, and even if he did, I felt pretty sure that he would understand that we were experiencing a Bad Air Alert inside the pickup.

Would he want the Head of Ranch Security eking out a miserable existence breathing stale air? Heck no. I was pretty certain that he would want me to share the window with him.

Even though I was following Slim's wishes on this deal, I had a feeling that I would need to do it in a . . . uh . . . how should I say this? In a stealthy manner, let us say. Slowly. Delicately. I mean, your ordinary run of low-class mutts wouldn't have given a thought to delicacy. They would have just blundered across the seat, plopped themselves in the driver's lap, and stuck their drippy mouths out the window.

That's not the way I do business. If we can't do

it properly, by George, we don't do it at all.

I began the procedure by studying Slim's fose in prayfile . . . face in profile, let us say. His mind seemed far away, lost in thought. This was good. I reached for the keypad of my mind and punched in the commands for a procedure we call Slow Creep. I began inching my enormous body across the seat while at the same time keeping a careful eye on Slim.

Pretty impressive, huh? You bet.

Slim suspected nothing, but I knew there was little chance that I could slip past Drover without provoking some kind of comment. Sure enough, when I tried to slither myself through the tiny space between him and the seat, he noticed.

"Where are you going?"

"Shhh, not so loud. My window's rolled up and I'm about to gag on the stale air."

"When I said that, you told me to count my blessings."

"Did you?"

"Yeah, I counted to one and quit."

"Well, do a recount. You must have missed something."

"Sunshine's all I could think of."

"There are more blessings, Drover, hundreds of them. You just have to look for them in all of

Life's crannies and nannies. Now, if you'll excuse me . . ."

At last, he moved out of the way. "Well, it doesn't seem fair that you always get the fresh air and I have to sit in the middle."

I heaved a sigh. "Okay, Drover, remember that little promotion we talked about? As of this moment, I am promoting you to the Shotgun Position."

His eyes lit up. "Oh goodie, Shotgun! I've always dreamed of riding Shotgun." He dashed over to the right side of the seat, and there his smile faded. "Yeah, but . . . the window's rolled up."

"Drover, I deal in large concepts, not tiny details. You'll just have to work it out for yourself."

I resumed my Stealthy Scoot across the seat. By this time, I had made contact with Slim's right leg. I paused and did another quick scan of his face. It came back negative, so I mushed on to the most delicate part of the procedure, entering the Lapalary Region of his lap. If a guy trips an alarm, this is where it happens, as he snail-crawls over that first leg and oozes himself toward the window, threading the upper portion of his body through, around, and between the driver's two arms.

It's a toughie, let me tell you, and there are very few dogs who can pull it off. What usually happens is that the dog gets careless, presses too hard, sets off the motion sensors, and gets tossed to the other side of the pickup.

But, heh heh, you'll be pleased to know that I pulled it off. After minutes and minutes of slow, delicate creeping, I oozed myself onto the Lapalary Region and plunged my nose into the stream of crisp, clean fall air. YES! Oh, sweet air! Oh, happy lungs! It was delicious, well worth all the pain and suffering I had endured to get there.

At that point, I moved rapidly into the next phase: resetting all the switches for Face, Tail, Ears, Eyes, and Mouth, and reconfiguring the system to produce an expression we call "I've Been Here All Day, No Kidding." That's a pretty important part of the procedure because, sooner or later, the driver is going to figure out that . . . well, he's got a dog in his lap. The idea is to have "I've Been Here" ready to roll.

It took Slim a while to respond, longer than I'd expected. I think I might have strung it out a little longer, but I made a poor calculation on Weight Distribution and pressed too hard with one of my hind paws. Also, I was sitting within the circle of his two arms, between his chest and the steering wheel, and I guess he was having a little trouble . . . well, seeing the road.

Don't forget, I'm a pretty big guy. Huge body, enormous shoulders, muscular thighs, the kind of body that causes the eyes of lady dogs to pop out of their heads.

Anyway, he noticed. "Hank, you're sitting in my lap."

Right. Yes. I was aware of that, and it was pretty touching, wasn't it? I mean, out of all the laps of all the cowboys in the whole world, I had chosen to sit on *his*. A cowboy and his loyal dog, going off to feed cattle. Very touching.

"I can't drive like this."

Oh? Well, gee, I'd been there all day . . . most of the day. He hadn't noticed?

"Reckon you could move?"

Well, I'd gone to quite a lot of trouble to get there, to be honest, and the air was really nice on his side of the pickup. So the bottom line was . . . no, I couldn't see that moving was a very good option. Not anytime soon. Maybe later.

"If I roll down the winder on your side, will you move?"

Actually . . . actually I was more and more impressed with the Air Quality on his side. It seemed fresher, cleaner, and sweeter than the air on the other side. It seemed better in every—

"Move!"

Yikes. Suddenly and all at once, he flexed his body muscles and sent me flying out of his lap. Gee whiz, he didn't need to be such a brute about it, I mean, if he'd wanted me to move, why hadn't he just come right out and said so? I could take a hint.

I tucked up my tail, lowered my ears, and beamed him an expression we call "Dog Rebuked." I was disappointed that it caused him to laugh.

"Do you want me to have a wreck and get us all killed?"

Well . . . no, since he put it like that.

Just then, something magical happened. By George, the Shotgun window rolled itself down! Slim noticed it too, and he said, "There. Stick your nose out that side . . . and Hank, try not to chop off your head. Remember them buttons."

Buttons? Why was everyone on the ranch talking about buttons? And what did Slim know about buttons anyway? He was a bachelor and I happened to know that half of the shirts he wore were missing at least one button.

I marched over to my window and shoved Drover onto the floor. "Time's up. Scram."

"Yeah, but . . . I thought I got a promotion."

"You've been fired."

"Fired! I just got here. What did I do?"

I beamed him a gaze of purest steel. "You've been wasting oxygen, Drover. You had your chance and you blew it. Sorry."

He whined and moaned, but I ignored him. I mean, oxygen is very precious and we couldn't allow him to go on squindering it.

I plunged my face and nose into the rushing river of fresh air, closed my eyes, and let the wind flap my ears and tongue, flutter my whiskers, and tickle my chin. OH YES! Fellers, this was very close to Life's True Meaning and Purpose.

And you know what? I decided that the air was sweeter on my side after all. If Slim wanted to be such a greedy goat, he could keep his old window . . . and ride the rest of the way without my warm presence in his lap.

Pretty stern punishment, huh? You bet, but these people have to learn.

CHAPTER TEN

My Head Gets
Cut Off

It took us maybe ten minutes to reach our next destination, the Dutcher Creek pasture. As we pulled across the cattle guard into the pasture, Slim said, "I wonder if that coyote'll be on the feed ground today." I gave him a blank stare, and he said, "There's been a coyote coming up to eat with the cows."

Oh yes, that story, but I didn't believe it. A coyote *eating feed* with the cows? Impossible.

Most of the cows had already come in to the feed ground and were waiting for us—waiting impatiently, I might add, milling, bawling, complaining, and staring at us with empty bovine expressions.

It's always a little irritating to see them doing this. I mean, a cow has nothing better to do than stand around on the feed ground and wait for somebody to deliver her groceries, right? If they thought our service was too slow, then why didn't they go eat the bark off a few trees? We'd fed them yesterday, but do you suppose they ever thanked us or showed even a shred of gratitude?

No sir. Cows never say thank you. They gibble what we gob them and bawl for more, as though they're starving to death. Well, they're not. They're all as fat as mud. You know the problem with cows? They have too much idle time and all they think about is food. Let 'em go get a job, that's what I say.

They *gobble* what we give them, is what I meant to say, not "gibble what we gobble them" or whatever it was. Givvle what we gob them.

Skip it.

We pulled up on the feed ground, an open space on the west side of the creek, and parked beneath some big cottonwood trees. Slim left the engine running, because that's what you're supposed to do with diesel engines in the wintertime, leave 'em running. You probably didn't know that, but it's true. Diesel engines run better when they're hot. Why? I have no idea, but Slim said so and that's good enough for me.

While we waited for the rest of the cows to come in, he pushed his hat at a downward angle so that the brim almost touched his nose, and scrunched down in the seat. I guess he noticed that Drover and I were staring at him. Why were we staring at him? No particular reason. We were just . . . well, waiting for something to happen.

"I'll bet y'all wish I'd sing you a song."

What? Was he joking? Have we ever discussed Slim's singing? Maybe not. See, when we're out doing something on the ranch, he makes up these corny songs, and what can a dog do but sit there and listen? It seems a little weird to me, a grown man singing to his dogs, but he's done it, not once, but many times.

He seems to think we love his so-called music. Ha. We put up with it, that's all, because we *have to,* because that's one of the things we have to do to keep our jobs.

He grinned. "Well, okay. If you'll sit up and beg, maybe I'll sing for you."

Oh, brother. This was so silly.

"See, I want to be sure y'all really love my singing. When you're a famous musician like me, you hate to perform for an audience of noodles. If you really love my singing, sit up and beg for a song."

Drover and I traded glances, and he whispered, "Is he kidding?"

"I don't think so. He wants us to go into the Begging Position."

"Should we do it?"

"We have no choice, Drover. We're trapped . . . unless you'd rather walk home."

"No, my feet hurt. Let's beg."

"I agree. Let's do the routine, listen to the tiresome thing, and get it over with. Surely it won't take too long."

We settled ourselves into the seat, raised our front paws, and became nice little beggars. It was embarrassing, but what can you do?

Slim nodded and grinned. "That's pretty good, and I'm really honored, but I think it might be better if you whined too. Can you whine for a song?"

Whine? No, absolutely not! I had never whined for a song in my whole life, and I wasn't fixing to start now.

I turned to Drover, who was sitting there like a little stooge with his paws in the air. "Cancel, abort. We're calling this thing off, Drover. It's just too ridiculous. We're going on strike."

And with that, we lowered our front paws and braced ourselves for the consequences. Would he kick us out? Make us walk home? I didn't care. We have our pride, you know, and a dog can stand only so much cowboy nonsense.

Slim's grin wilted. "You ain't going to give me a whine?"

No sir, no whines. Not today, not ever. If he wanted an audience of whiners, he should sing to a cat.

"Dumb dogs. Y'all just don't appreciate real talent."

This was so childish. I couldn't believe he was doing it.

He shrugged. "Oh well, I couldn't think of a song anyway."

See? He'd put us through all that nonsense, and he didn't even have a song to sing! This was outrageous.

He looked off to the west and sat up in the seat. He was staring at something. "I'll be derned. There she is, that same coyote."

This I had to see for myself. I pushed Drover aside, marched over to the left window, stepped up into Slim's lap, and peered off to the west.

"Watch where you're stepping, bozo."

Sorry.

Slim pointed into the distance. "Look yonder. See her on the edge of those cows? She's a pretty little thing, has a nice coat of hair, and looks healthy. She's waiting for me to toss her some feed."

I narrowed my eyes and focused them on the edge of the herd. Sure enough, there she was. So it was true. This wasn't just another one of Slim's

windy tales. She stood off to herself, watching us with a steady coyote gaze. And, yes, she was kind of pretty.

I looked closer. She was very pretty.

I leaned against the window ledge. She was *gorgeous*! And suddenly my mind was flooded with a torrent of fragrant memories from long ago. Holy smokes, do you realize who that was? You won't believe this, so hang on.

IT WAS MISSY COYOTE!

Missy Coyote, the lovely coyote princess, the woman of my dreams, my one and only true love! At one point in my career, I had given serious thought to throwing it all away, joining up with the coyotes, becoming a professional cannibal, and marrying Missy. That hadn't quite worked out, but, wowee, here she was again!

My whole body trembled with . . . something. Excitement. Delight. I wasn't sure I could contain myself . . . and I didn't. I lost it right there.

Aaaaah-ooooooo! Aaaaaaa-ooooooo!

"Hank, dry up, you'll scare her off."

Dry up? Was he joking? Can you dry up a mighty river that rushes to the sea? He could forget about me drying up. I was too far gone for that. I hopped my front paws up on the armrest and reloaded my air tanks for another Announcement of Love.

"*Aaaaa-ooooo! Aaaaaa* . . . SQUEAK! GULK! GORK!*"

You won't believe this. **The window glass had just rolled up on my neck!**

"HARK! HONK! ARG! HELP!"

Was I going to just stand there while that thing chopped off my head? Heck no. I did what any brave, strong, red-blooded American cowdog would have done: I braced my feet against the armrest and went to Full Reverse on all engines, and we're talking about claws that were . . .

"Hank, hold still, you've got your neck in the winder!"

. . . throwing up sparks and hunks of solid concrete. *Did he need to tell me my neck was caught in the window?* Hey, it was *my* neck and I knew exactly what was happening to it, and if he thought I was going to "hold still" while the window cut of my head, he was nuts.

I thrashed and struggled, but . . . GULK! GORP!—the window pressed tighter, ever tighter, around my . . . GURP!—throatalary region.

"Hank, get away from the button, you're making it worse!"

Buttons! Did I care about his buttons? My head was getting cut off!

SNORP! GASP! WHEEZE! . . .

Suddenly it was over—not my life, but the ordeal. It happened fast. One second I was thrashing wildly against the deadly grisp of the window's grasp, and the next second . . . well, I was flying backward across the seat at a high rate of speed. My neck was free, my life was saved, and I sure gave Drover a plowing. We both ended up on the floorboard in a heap.

Maybe you think I destroyed the window or jerked the door right off its hinges. Good guess, but the tooth is even stranger than friction. See, somehow in middle of the crisis, the terrible crisis, the window rolled itself down again, saving my life by the narrowest of margins.

The cab of the pickup fell into an eerie silence. Nobody said a word. Slim looked at the backs of his hands. They showed . . . uh . . . long red marks, perhaps scratches. Okay, maybe I'd scratched him up a little bit.

His eyes came at me like bullets. "Good honk, did you have to claw me half to death?"

I was being decafinated. What did he expect? Decapitated.

"And lookie here. You tore my shirt."

Shirt? He was worried about *his shirt*?

He opened the door and stepped outside.

"Get out of my pickup, you meathead, and don't ever set foot in it again!"

Fine with me, buddy! The sooner I got out of that dog-killer pickup, the quicker I would keep my head where it was supposed to be.

I slinked . . . slank . . . slunk . . . across the seat and dived out the door, one step ahead of the boot he aimed at my tail section.

"Now get in the back and try to act your age, not your IQ."

See how he is? One little rip in his shirt and he was ready to plunge our relationship back into another Period of Darkness. Anger. Insults. Irrational behavior. I don't know how you please these people.

Okay, I admit that he'd suffered a few gouges on his hands, but don't forget whose neck had almost been amputated.

I leaped up into the back of the pickup, sat down near the front, and began sulking. Yes, I sulked and I was proud to be sulking. It was the right and proper thing to . . . wait a second, hold everything. Had you forgotten who was out there in the pasture?

I'd forgotten. I mean, when the pickup had tried to cut off my head, I'd been forced to turn all my attention to the crisis at hand, and I'd completely forgotten about . . .

I leaped up and rushed to the rear of the pickup. There, I watched a strange scene unfoil. Slim opened up one of the feed sacks and scooped out a double handful of cake (that's pelleted feed, don't forget). He tossed a couple of pieces of cake toward the coyote. She sniffed the air, sniffed the ground, and walked toward the spot where the cake had fallen.

She followed her nose until she found the first piece, took it in her mouth, and began crunching it up. Slim nodded and smiled and tossed her several more pieces.

Amazing! Do you realize how unusual this was? Coyotes are creatures of the wild and they never come around people. They don't like people, are scared of 'em, and always run away. Yet here was Missy Coyote . . . eating cake!

"*Aaaaaaa-oooooo!*"

Slim shot me a frown. "Hank, hush. Let 'er eat."

Right. I'd let 'er eat . . . tomorrow. She had the rest of her life to eat cake, but right now, she was fixing to get reacquainted with Hank the . . .

You won't believe this. I couldn't believe it. Guess who was already on his way out into the pasture to meet my coyote princess. I'll give you a hint. It wasn't Slim.

CHAPTER ELEVEN

Missy Coyote Falls Madly in Love with Me

D rover. Little Mister Buttinski. I should have
known. He always does this. He's not smart
enough or bold enough to find a girl of his own, so
he's always trying to horn in on my deals.

Well, I was fixing to put a stop to that nonsense. I leaped out of the back of the pickup and
went streaking out to greet the lady of my . . .

Have we mentioned that cows will sometimes
chase a dog? It's true, and we need to talk about
that. See, when a dog makes an appearance in a
herd of cows, there's always a dummy or two that
will chase him around and make threatening ges-
tures with her horns. But here's the crazy part.

See, cows chase dogs because they mistake the dog for a prowling coyote, because cows don't like coyotes.

Do you see where this is leading? Missy Coyote had come right up to the edge of the herd and the cows hadn't paid her any mind, but when the Head of Ranch Security entered the scene, they thought I was a coyote, and came hunting ME! That gives you some idea of just how DUMB they are. Incredible. I couldn't believe it.

Well, I couldn't believe it until that big Hereford cow scooped me up on her horns and flang me about twenty feet into the air. At that point, I had no choice but to believe it. Glaring down at her from high above the feed ground, I yelled, "Moron, I work here! I'm the guy who protects you from—"

BAM!

The, uh, ground rushed up to meet me, terrible wreck, and no ordinary dog could have . . . COUGH . . . walked away from it. But I'm no quitter. I not only walked away from it, I *ran* away from it because . . . well, because that same hateful witch came after me again, snorting steam and throwing hooks with her horns.

For a second, I faced her and gave her a

savage burst of barking. "Idiot! I'm not a coyote! I'm the Head of . . ."

Anyway, I've already admitted that I, uh, retired from the battlefield, so to speak. Okay, I ran for my life, which was no disgrace. It was just a little embarrassing, since I was trying to impress a lady.

Why hadn't the cows chased Drover? He'd scampered right through the middle of them and they hadn't even raised a moo. Did that make sense? No. It made no sense at all. I mean, first they'd had a chance to direct their nastiness toward Missy, a genuine wild coyote who was eating their food, and then they'd had a perfect shot at Buttinski.

They'd passed up both chances, but when the Protector of Their Ranch had ventured forth . . . oh well. Cows are dumb, that's all you can say.

I turned on an amazing burst of speed and left the hateful cow eating my dust. How foolish of her to think she could chase down a top of the line, blue ribbon cowdog! And at that point, with all the distractions out of the way, I altered course and streaked over to the princess of my dreams.

Wow! She was even more beautiful than I remembered: long fluffy tail, silky fur coat, sharp tapered nose, pointed ears. Wow! Unfortunately, she was being distracted by my former friend and assistant (I'd already decided to fire him), so she wasn't able to appreciate the full effect of my manly swagger.

Ten feet away, I could hear Drover making a fool of himself. "Gosh, I've never met a real princess before. I've heard about 'em in fairy tales and I've always wanted to meet one. I'm so

114

thrilled and excited, I don't know what to say."

Missy didn't know what to say either. She seemed puzzled and slightly amused by his breathless presentation. "Little white dog have name?"

"Oh yeah, sure, I almost forgot." He grinned and rolled his eyes up at her. "I'm Drover."

"Drover work on big ranch with Hunk?"

"Oh yeah. Well, he kind of works for me." He fluttered his stub tail. "I'm a pretty important dog, and I was wondering . . . would you be my girlfriend?"

I got there just in time to save her from this shameless fraud. I shoved my way past Drover. "Out of the way, you little thief, and how dare you try to steal my girl!"

"Well, I just—"

"Go to your room! Immediately."

"It's back at the ranch."

"Then scram. Get lost. Go scratch a flea." I inserted my enormous body between the runt and the lady, and gave her a sultry smile. "Ah, sweet Missy Coyote! How often hast thou visited me in slumberous sleep, filling the empty cave of my dreams with glorious sunlight and rainbowed visions!"

Drover poked his head into the conversation.

"That's what I was fixing to say."

I pushed him away. "Missy, my ky-up coat cake . . . my coyote cupcake, I've hardly slept a wink since these eyes last feasted upon the prime rib of thy beauty."

Drover appeared again. "That's not true, Missy. He slept all night last night, and I heard him talking in his sleep . . . about Beulah the Collie!"

I whirled around and showed him a mouthful of fangs. "Will you shut your trap! What's wrong with you?"

"Well, when I saw her, I just fell in love. I can't help myself."

"Drover, you're not in love, you're in-sane. Go away." I pushed him into the background and turned to the lovely lady. "I don't know who this guy is, Missy. I've never seen him before. He's an impostor."

She seemed puzzled. "Not Hunk's friend?"

"He's . . . okay, we used to be friends, but that's all gone by the hayside. He's fired, history. He'll never work on this ranch again. The important thing right now is"—I wiggled my left eyebrow—"I'm here. And you're here. And we're both here. And, well, here we are."

She chirped a little laugh. "Hunk talk funny all the time, make Missy laugh."

"I'm sorry to hear that. I mean, I'm trying to be very sincere, even romantic."

"What means . . . 'rumantic'?"

"I'm glad you asked, Missy. It means . . .

Somehow Drover managed to worm his way between my legs and suddenly he popped up, between us. "It means I'm in love!"

Okay, that did it. I was one second away from giving the little tuna the thrashing he so richly deserved, when suddenly the blare of the pickup horn sounded in the distance. Then Slim called out, "Come on, dogs, the train's fixing to leave! Load up or walk."

Load up or walk? Ha. That was the easiest decision of the year. For his information, I had much better things to do than ride around with him in a booby-trapped pickup. I turned my adoring gaze back on . . .

Huh?

She was gone! The horn must have scared her away. And you know who else was gone? I whirled around and went charging off to the north. "Drover, come back here! If I ever get my paws on you . . ."

I topped a little hill and saw them in the distance, walking toward the canyon country off to the north. Drover was beside her, the little . . . he would pay for this! I turned on an amazing burst of speed and caught up with them. As I approached, I could hear Drover spouting poetry, if you can believe that.

"Oh gosh, Missy Coyote, your face is
    delicious,
I wish I could make it a sandwich
With mayonnaise and pickles and mustard
    and bread.
I think that the taste would be grandwich."

I knifed in between them and gave Drover Full Fangs. "That poem was pathetic, Drover. It was the worst garbage I ever heard."

"Well, it rhymed. I thought it was pretty good."

"Comparing the face of a lovely princess to a sandwich? That's sick, Drover. I'm shocked and dismayed. Furthermore, your rhyme was awful—sandwich and grandwich."

"Well, I couldn't think of anything else that would rhyme with 'sandwich.'"

"Never mind. I'll deal with you later." I turned

back to Missy. "I'm sorry, ma'am, we've had this trouble before. Just ignore him. He's a lunatic."

"What means, 'lunatic'?"

'It means he's unbalanced. Unhinged. Immature. Much too childish to be . . . where are we going?"

"Missy must go back to coyote billage."

"Ah, great. So I'll walk you home. That sounds romantic, doesn't it?"

"Not so rumantic if Scraunch come along and find Hunk."

"Who? Oh, him. Your big ugly brother? Ha ha. Don't give it a thought, my prairie wildflower. The way I'm feeling right now, old Scraunch wouldn't stand a chance."

"Scraunch pretty bad fellow."

"He smells bad, Missy, but I can always hold my nose. Ha ha." She didn't appreciate the humor. "Okay, we'll keep an eye out for Scraunch. Drover, I'm assigning you to guard duty."

"Me? Yeah, but—"

"That's a direct order. Make yourself scarce and keep an eye out for a big ugly coyote."

He hung his head. "Oh darn. I wanted to—"

"Hush. We don't want to hear about your problems." I turned back to Missy. "So you like poetry, huh? Well, you'll be thrilled to know that my poems are ten times better than Drover's wilted rhymes. Here, give a listen to this one.

"Oh Missy, my princess, your face is just
    awesome.
It's not like a sandwich, I say.
See, Drover writes worse than a dim-witted
    possum.
His poems are sure to dismay.

"I, on the other hand, write from the heart,
My verses are pure and sincere.
I say that your face is more lovely than art,
And Drover's a pain in the rear."

I shot a glance to see if she had been swept away on a tidal wave of emotion. Apparently not. She gave me a puzzled look. "Missy not understand about sandwich and possum. Sound berry strange."

"I see. Well, I'm sorry you missed the deep emotional message in my poem, so let's move along to something else. Would you be thrilled to know that I write songs? And would you be completely blown away if I sang a love song, just for you? Of course you would. Here, listen to this."

And with that, I belted out a terrific love song.

CHAPTER TWELVE

This Ending Will Knock Your Socks Off

Walking with My Honey

Walking along, just my honey and me, on a
    warm sunny winter's day.
Walking her home, just the two of us, having
    fun along the way.
I give her a wink, she gives me a smile,
I want to stretch it out another country mile.
Walking with my honey back to Coyote Town,
    everything's going to be okay.

Walking along, Missy Coyote and me, I've got
    a feeling that is hard to believe.

I feel ten feet tall and eight feet deep, and,
    man, it's getting harder to breathe!
She's walking her dog, I'm walking my sweet,
We can hear the little birdies singing "tweet,
    tweet, tweet."
Walking with my honey back to Coyote Town
    and wishing she'd never leave.

Walking along just as slow as we can, did I
    notice that she gave me a grin?
I think she did and it's plain to see that
    Hank's about to win.
How 'bout a little kiss? It'll never show.
Your cannibal brother doesn't need to know.
Walking with my honey back to Coyote Town,
    and hoping it'll never end.

Pretty incredible love song, huh? You bet. It
was certainly one of the best I'd ever composed
and performed for a lovely lady. But the question
remained—would it sweep Missy Coyote completely off her feet and cause her to smother me
with love and kisses?

I heaved a sigh and looked deeply into her . . .
you know, there's something a little unsettling
about a woman with yellow eyes. Let's be frank. I

had looked into the yellow eyes of her brothers, cousins, and cannibal friends, and hadn't exactly been warmed by the experience. Her yellow eyes brought back a rush of memories that weren't so sweet, memories that caused the hair along my spine to stand up, and little termites of fear to crawl on the back of my neck.

On the other hand, I wasn't the kind of dog who allowed himself to be a slave to first impressions. So she had yellow eyes that were . . . well, a little creepy? I was mature enough to look deeper, and to see the goodness and beauty that dwelled below the surface.

Anyway, I looked deeply into her unblinking yellow gaze. "Well, Missy, what do you say about that? Great song, huh?"

She gave me a shy smile. "So Hunk want kiss from Missy?"

For a second, I couldn't breathe. "Well, I suppose . . . yes! Absolutely."

She glanced over her shoulders. "What about Scraunch?"

"He's your brother, Missy, but that doesn't mean I want to kiss him."

"No, no. What if Scraunch come along and see us?"

At that very moment, guess who showed up,

squeaking and hopping around. Drover. "Hank, we need to talk!"

"Some other time. I'm busy."

"C-c-coyotes!"

"Of course she's a coyote."

Suddenly Missy whirled around and whispered, "Hunk must leave! Scraunch coming!"

HUH?

I turned and saw . . . YIPES!! Fifteen big scruffy cannibals came boiling over the top of a little hill. They saw us and let out a chorus of blood-chilling howls. In the lead was Missy's . . . gulp . . . have we ever described Scraunch? Big guy, real big. Huge. Jaws like a bear trap, teeth like a shark, eyes that glowed in the dark.

Gulp.

I turned back to Missy. "Would you think it cowardly of me if I, uh, left you here? I mean, we have cattle to feed and patrols to do."

"Hunk leave now! Run!"

"Well, if you're sure . . ."

She leaned forward and planted a delicious kiss on my mouth. "Hunk go back to ranch now! Run, run, run!"

For a moment, I was lost in a fog of perfume, but then . . . uh oh, the mob was coming closer. They were yelling, hooting, and howling about all

the terrible things they were going to inflict on my . . .

"Drover, I don't want to alarm you, but we need to be leaving."

"Help! This leg's killing me!

"On the count of three, we will launch all dogs and set a speed course back to the pickup. Ready? One!"

ZOOM!

He was gone, a little white rocket moving across the prairie at the speed of light. And there was nothing wrong with his leg.

I tossed one last wistful gaze at my coyote princess, faced into the wind, and went to Full Throttle on all engines. I left my True Love in a cloud of dust, and left the coyote army choking on the fumes of my rocket engines.

Slim was driving away when we got there and maybe he thought he was going to leave us afoot. Ha! There was no chance of that, not with Scraunch and all his buddies on our trail. No sir. I barked and dived in front of the pickup and even threatened to rip off the tires if he didn't pull that thing over. I guess that scared him pretty badly, and finally he stopped and got out.

Of course he had to make a few smart

remarks. "I ain't running a taxi service. You want a ride or not?"

Oh yes, no question about that . . . and could we hurry?

"Well, you ain't riding up front with me. Get in the back."

Fine. No problem there. Who wanted to ride in that head-chopping pickup anyway? Not me.

He let down the tailgate and we dogs went flying into the back, ran straight to the front and went into our Bunker Positions. I didn't figure the coyotes would jump into the back of a pickup, but a dog should never take chances. When in doubt, head for the bunkers.

But you'll be proud to know that once we got moving, I climbed out of my bunker and delivered one last barrage of barking to the coyotes.

"Hey, Scraunch, I kissed your sister! What do you say about that, huh? And next time, I'll kiss her *twice,* and if you don't like it, you can go sit on a tack! Ha."

It was a huge moral victory for the Security Division, which only goes to prove . . . well, if you're going to mouth off to a cannibal, do it from a moving pickup.

When we got back to headquarters, Slim

kicked us out. "I've got three more pastures to feed and y'all can't go. Too many clowns can spoil a circus. When I get my old pickup back, we'll be hiring dogs again."

Gee, what got him in such a snit? Oh well.

For two long days, Slim fed cattle by himself. Then, on Wednesday morning, he left the ranch at 6:30, drove the Booby-Trapped Pickup into town, and returned around 9:00, driving the old junk heap we had all come to love and respect. It smelled bad, it smoked and wheezed, it rattled and clanged, but it was our old pickup—and it didn't have guillotine windows.

And that's about it. Drover and I got our jobs back and Slim got his dogs back. I had survived the Booby-Trapped Pickup, won the heart of Missy Coyote, and cleaned house on the entire Coyote Army. Oh, happy day! Life was good again.

Fellers, it doesn't get any better than that. This case is closed.

Have you read all of Hank's adventures?

Join Hank the Cowdog's Security Force

Are you a big Hank the Cowdog fan? Then you'll want to join Hank's Security Force. Here is some of the neat stuff you will receive:

Welcome Package
- A Hank paperback of your choice
- A free Hank bookmark

Eight issues of The Hank Times newspaper
- Stories about Hank and his friends
- Lots of great games and puzzles
- Special previews of future books
- Fun contests

More Security Force Benefits
- Special discounts on Hank books and audiotapes
- An original Hank poster (19" x 25") absolutely free
- Unlimited access to Hank's Security Force website at www.hankthecowdog.com

Total value of the Welcome Package and *The Hank Times* is $23.95. However, your two-year membership is **only $8.95** plus $4.00 for shipping and handling.

- -

☐ Yes, I want to join Hank's Security Force. Enclosed is $12.95 ($8.95 + $4.00 for shipping and handling) for my **two-year membership**. [Make check payable to Maverick Books. International shipping extra.]

WHICH BOOK WOULD YOU LIKE TO RECEIVE IN YOUR WELCOME PACKAGE? CHOOSE ANY BOOK IN THE SERIES. _____

_____ **BOY or GIRL**
YOUR NAME   (CIRCLE ONE)

_____
MAILING ADDRESS

_____
CITY   STATE   ZIP

_____
TELEPHONE   BIRTH DATE
_____ Are you a ☐ Teacher or ☐ Librarian?
E-MAIL

Send check or money order for $12.95 to:

Hank's Security Force   **DO NOT SEND CASH.**
Maverick Books   **OFFER SUBJECT TO CHANGE.**
P.O. Box 549   *Allow 3–4 weeks for delivery.*
Perryton, Texas 79070

The Hank the Cowdog Security Force, the Welcome Package, and The Hank Times *are the sole responsibility of Maverick Books. They are not organized, sponsored, or endorsed by Penguin Group (USA) Inc., Puffin Books, Viking Children's Books, or their subsidiaries or affiliates.*